DOUBLE ECHO

BY THE SAME AUTHOR

Die nag het net een oog (1991)
Die duiwel se tuin (1993)
Koue soen (1994)
Bloedbroer (1995)
Storieboek (1996)
Mooidraai Basuin (1997)
Nagbesoeker (1997)
Hostis (1998)
Klipgooi (1999)
'n Tweede asem vir Jan A (2001)
Spinnerak (2006)
Jagseisoen (2007)
Rooi Luiperd (2008)
Harde woorde (2009)
Afspraak in Venesië (2009)
Die onbekendes (2010)
Die Genesis-faktor (2010)
Helse manier van koebaai sê (2011)
Jy-weet-wie (2012)
Moord in die beloofde land (2013)
Pad na jou hart (2013)
Die vierde stem (2014)
Vir altyd (2015)

1

Just another day. True, it was wet after yesterday's dry spell, and yes, he had moved on, but as on so many other mornings he didn't have the vaguest notion where he would be spending the night.

Above him the grey heavens spread out. While the rain had not yet started there was just enough moisture in the air to keep his cheeks damp, plaster his hair to his forehead and send a chilly trickle down his neck.

Just another road.

So many of them already.

He was wearing a leather jacket over his black T-shirt. Jeans. Comfortable shoes; walking shoes. The remainder of his clothes were in his backpack and the suitcase he had in his left hand.

But he was carrying far more than that, of course.

His name was Paul Mullan and he was thirty-four years old.

As the train had crawled into Wellington station half an hour previously, he remembered once reading that all trains had to stop there. He had a ticket for Cape Town, but seeing as it was just another junction and almost certainly not a destination, he was free to hop off should he have the inclination. The inclination arrived; he went with it.

On the platform he was alone with the rustling, pale-brown leaves.

In the gents he had held his breath while making use of one of the country's most dubious urinals. Next he set off for the little café, where he bought something for his rumbling stomach from the semi-comatose cashier. Due to the lack of alternatives he walked away with a styrofoam tub of slap chips covered in grubby cling wrap. The chips no longer really qualified as *slap*, their advanced state of rigor mortis suggesting they had been fried the previous day, if not before that. But it was just ever so slightly better than nothing. Outside the station, chewing as he went, he walked past a tangle of early-morning boozers sitting and philosophising on the broken tar.

Then he had to make a choice: the Railway Hotel with its roof of rusty corrugated iron was not an option, which meant he had to decide between taking a right to cross the bridge into Wellington, or carrying on straight and leaving town.

The road ahead appeared to be in good condition. Sometimes a simple fact like that makes up your mind.

And so there he was on the R44.

The inclement weather did not detract from the natural beauty that surrounded him: so many shades of green, graceful hills, mountains made for wondering at. Space. Paul Mullan would have liked to believe that space could make a difference, and that somewhere close by a solution might lie waiting, a solution that had escaped him in the frenetic bustle of Pretoria. But there had already been other expanses, and other cities, and a variety of weather conditions, and he was still just as screwed as when he had started his journey.

But who knew. The alternative was to stop dead, and then he would lose it.

There was no sound other than his even paces on the hard shoulder –

or yes, if he opened his ears to it: the swoop of wings, a bird seeking shelter, or so he imagined; something rustling in the bushes nearby, maybe a small animal hiding from him; the wind, rasping wistfully; and a ... car approaching. His hand shot out, well rehearsed, thumb up, even though he didn't expect it to stop.

Sure enough, they pressed on, a family in a white Yaris. There was just enough time for his keen sight to pick up the shape of two large heads in the front and three smaller ones in the back, and then the car disappeared behind the sign.

R46	Hermon	10
R44	Porterville	63
R46	Ceres	64

Each of these places seemed like a valid option, or equally not.

He kept walking, passing turn-offs to farms and nurseries. There were no other cars. It seemed that everyone in the district already was where they needed to be.

To his right the area's characteristic greenery was absent, having yielded to grey veld in which clusters of sheep huddled miserably, well-padded rumps in the air. To the left things looked as they were meant to, a lush green. Long wires supported by tall posts snaked across the contours, staking their claim in the name of modernity. Of course, the neatly parcelled land already signified human intervention, but unlike the stark rigidity of the power lines it seemed *right*, as if nature had accepted the orderly alterations.

About eight kilometres further he saw a turn-off to the left. In the way that some people develop an internal clock, he had grown an odometer. If he walked at a set pace, he knew how long it would take him to reach a particular spot in the distance.

Time for another decision. Straight, towards Ceres, or should he go and see what lay to the left?

What difference would it make? He had no idea why he was hesitating. It was as if his senses had sharpened and he could hear more than was audible to others. Could feel something extra in the air, too.

That was it. He frowned. Had he believed in such a thing as a sixth sense, he would have thought that it was now trying to convince him not to follow the turning. Straight ahead would be better. He had never been to Ceres and it was as good a place as any.

But, just to prove to himself that he paid no heed to something as unreliable as a premonition, he left the R44.

R46

Hermon	1
Riebeek-Kasteel	10
Malmesbury	30

Walking gives you plenty of time to think. Too much. But he was here to think. This was Operation Clear Your Mind.

He thought of the people he had left behind. Leaving them was an insult, because they had wanted to help. Nobody had a grudge against him.

He'd had to think of what to do next. New job, new place to stay. Now he couldn't imagine that he would stick anywhere, put down roots, even though in the past, just like so many people, he had gone looking for such a place and found it. Had found the right vocation too, but he was done with that forever.

His mind wouldn't clear.

He made his way over a bridge, looked down onto a swollen river, took a bend in the road, left the village of Hermon further behind. By now he pretty much knew he was more than four and less than five kilometres from the turn-off. His eye followed the rise of the hills up to where they turned to mountains far in the distance. Maybe he would have to call it a day around there, as his legs were growing tired, his soles feeling tender.

He wondered what still differentiated him from a hobo – the belief that he would, after all, give up walking one day? Who said most hobos didn't try to convince themselves of the same? At least he was getting to see the country.

Swartland. Winelands.

The sun squeezed through a break in the clouds. Here, nature put on even more of a display than before, and he wanted to absorb all the beauty, because how could he, now in his mid-thirties, be blind to it? He had to remember his life was far from over. He had been searching so long, struggling, filled with remorse. Finding nothing, because no salvation was to be found in external means, as any psychologist or indeed any self-help manual could have told him. The answer lies inside, people are your own personal hell, a road is a road, blah-blah-blah.

Then the sun was gone. Dark spots appeared on the tar ahead of him and around him.

The drops started coming down with more urgency.

And then, a car!

He didn't turn around as the hum of the engine grew louder. The vehicle would drive past, he knew, because even a Good Samaritan at the wheel would feel he was gliding down here too merrily, and why stop for some hapless fool who would only spoil the upholstery with his sodden arse? It would be expensive upholstery, too, as the engine sounded like it belonged to a BMW or a Mercedes.

Nevertheless, he shot out his arm, thumb pointing up.

A Mercedes. First the flash of silver metal, then a glimpse of a pair of hands on the steering wheel. The driver was in uniform. Paul just about raised his eyebrows in response; after all, how often did you see such a thing as a chauffeur these days? Well, sometimes, but *here*? The man, wearing a cap of the same light grey as his jacket, turned his head slightly, looking at him out of the corner of his eye, and Paul thought it might be his weariness that made him believe he could in that one instant discern an air of superiority in the way he looked away, chin up.

Upon spying the older man in a dark suit in the back, Paul decided he had not been imagining things, because *his* glance certainly qualified as haughty.

And there went the silver symbol of wealth, sailing to some or other destination where no doubt there was a fire crackling in the hearth, the most expensive brandy waiting to be poured and an electric blanket heating the king-size bed.

If such things could bring happiness, Paul was wishing for them now.

With annoyance he realised he still had his arm out.

Then he heard it.

The sound.

In a split second he was back *there*, that night, in the hour from which he cannot escape, no matter how far his feet carry him.

It was as if a great hand had grabbed him by the chest, thrust itself deep inside to find his heart and squeezed, squeezed. He couldn't breathe.

Two fainter sounds followed, the silence of the valley having been brutally suspended. Its serenity had been a mere illusion.

One shot. Two echoes.

2

Not a shot, he had to tell himself. Not a shot. Even though his heart was still thumping in his chest, his breathing not yet restored.

Shot.

Echo.

Echo.

A way ahead of him, but not all that far away, the Mercedes stood on the roadside. Safely brought to a stop.

Pull. Yourself. Together.

He set off again.

The chauffeur, in his pale-grey cap, jacket and trousers (black shoes, at least), got out to survey the damage. The rear right tyre was flat. His body language spoke of frustration, undoubtedly worsened by the fact that his uniform was being drenched. He got back in the car and closed the door.

Paul got closer, reached the car and started walking past. He wouldn't make a display of his Schadenfreude, even though he was recalling the fable of the tortoise and the hare.

'That's what you get, don't you think?'

Both windows on the driver's side were halfway down, but it wasn't the chauffeur speaking. The question had come from the back. The man would have made a good bass in some choir, had his voice been more melodic.

Paul stopped. 'Meaning?'

Irony in the intonation: 'If the bastards don't want to stop for you, they'll be forced to! How about you help us?'

'You mean like you helped me?'

'Better than we did, of course.' The man gestured towards the chauffeur. 'Johnny is still quite dry, but you're soaked already ... Johnny, greet the man.'

With *just* enough civility, he said, 'Good day.'

'Good day,' Paul answered incidentally, then asked the man at the back, 'And you, to whom am I speaking?'

'Bernard Russell. And you are?'

Paul gave him a good look over. He appeared to be in his mid-sixties, but he could have been younger. Or maybe it was his bold manner that gave him an energetic air. His shoulders were broad, as was his chest, filling the dark jacket. White shirt, blue tie with a precise knot. The angular face displayed no fat on the cheeks and none under the chin either. Everything was strong – the mouth, which could have been wider, the nose, the cheekbones, the eyes as dark as the suit the man was wearing. The grey in his black hair didn't detract from the package; rather, it was a distinguishing feature.

'Paul Mullan. Bernard, you look to me like the kind of person who is used to other people doing things for him.'

The chauffeur couldn't stand it. 'There's no need to beg him for help. The rain will stop any moment, and then I'll change the tyre.'

'No one is begging, Johnny. And no one is telling anyone what to do.' Bernard Russell waited for the reprimand to hit home before he continued. 'I think our friend will get it done more quickly than you. Paul, are you going anywhere in particular?'

Now *there's* a question for you.

'Hardly.'

'Then I think we could do each other a favour.' The man sounded pleased, in a formal way, as if he were in a boardroom where a point of conflict had just been resolved with an elementary compromise. 'You help me, then I help you.'

Paul was on the brink of becoming annoyed. 'I don't need money.'

'Time is money, and I'm asking for your time. But mainly I'm talking about a plate of good food and shelter for the night. So, what do you think?'

In such weather the offer would have been attractive to many a weary traveller, but Paul Mullan heard more than the words being spoken. The offer would mean that at least for tonight he wouldn't have to shut the door of yet another impersonal hotel or guest house behind him – after eating, as always, at a lonely little table while everyone wondered what the young man was doing all on his own. He couldn't say where the sudden need for company, for contact, was coming from, and he wondered whether he really wanted to spend time with these two cranks, but still, it was there.

He nodded.

Though Johnny didn't quibble any further, he was clearly one of those people who specialised in gestures and attitude. There was a Fuck You to his way of getting out of the car and a Fuck You to his opening the boot to retrieve the spare wheel, and an even more resounding Fuck You in the way he passed it to Paul. His slender, almost skinny face was expressionless, but perhaps the lines between his nose and mouth weren't always that deep; they were only so now because a stranger was doing his work, a stranger was part of the display of power into which the older man had converted the situation. The corners of Johnny's mouth turned downwards naturally; he had the kind of mouth you get from eating too much jam with a wooden spoon, thought Paul.

There was something absurd about the tyre-changing, and Paul viewed it the way someone else might: him, hunched over and working away, Johnny holding an umbrella over him at Bernard's command while trying to stay dry himself, with Bernard, who hadn't left the car, observing them from his throne.

'Progress ...?' the deep voice asked through the back window after a while.

'If you had bothered to get out, Bernard,' Paul answered, 'you wouldn't have to ask how I'm doing.'

He noticed Johnny stiffen. Not his mother's most attractive child. In fact, it was starting to seem to Paul as if the guy's mother must have done something untoward with a meerkat.

There was a chuckle from the car. It seemed that Russell enjoyed his lack of subservience, but Johnny, who wouldn't dare attempt the same, wasn't enjoying it in the least.

Things could get interesting, Paul thought, and added, 'But as long as you're sitting comfortably, it's all just dandy.'

3

Through the window he watched a long, never-ending ribbon of green. Splashes of brown and yellow cropped up too, and while a greyness the colour of the ocean on a stormy day still hung over everything, it was mostly green, green, in all its nuances. The area must have had plenty of rain, and the earth was making a great show of its gratitude.

He preferred sizing up his environment this way while he was being sized up. He was sitting across from Johnny No-last-name, whose attention was seemingly on his driving but was, Paul believed, taking notice of his every movement. Behind him was Bernard Russell, and it felt like the older man's eyes had been resting on the back of his head for so long he might expect to find a bald spot singed into it.

No talking. Paul imagined that there hadn't been much talking earlier either, and that this was most likely how the driving went. Johnny's words would be few; Bernard's more plentiful because talking is a way of demanding attention, but what did come out would always be something he first judged worthy of being said.

Riebeek-Kasteel, announced a sign.

They drove past the turn-off on the right. Paul saw the church tower reaching up into the sky; it had to be a breathtaking specimen if you were a church-tower aficionado. It reminded him of his childhood: small town, small existence.

He couldn't shake his discomfort. It wasn't that what he was wearing was so at odds with what the other two had on. It wasn't the distance in social standing between him and the man behind him, because he took no notice of such things. Life was unfair, and that was that. Russell had, ten to one, been born into luxury, and thanks to good investments his money would just keep growing, while the poor wouldn't have arseholes if shit was worth a cent.

Seeing as he couldn't put his finger on the cause, he thought he might as well try to relax. He knew he *looked* relaxed; he had long mastered the art of body language. He had to take this disruption of his routine as it came: a necessary change of pace before it was back to just him and the open road in the morning.

Flowers, shrubs, trees, hills, mountains.

Then the engine changed to a lower tune as Johnny slowed down for the next turn-off – in other words they weren't heading for Malmesbury.

Journey's End, read the sign. Somewhat less than that as far as he was concerned, Paul mused; more like Journey's Brief Interruption.

Dirt road. Krrr-krrr said the tyres, and pebbles shot up against the chassis like popping corn. Vineyard to the left, avenue of poplars, everything top-notch, not just your average farm.

He kept waiting for a small frisson of excitement. It should have been part of this unexpected situation in which he had landed, as would be the case with other people, but despite the presence of these two rather interesting characters he felt nothing. Maybe he'd lost the potential for it.

Another kilometre on and there it was, formidable as he might have expected, grand and expansive. It was a double-storey home, somewhat hidden among oak trees. The architecture seemed Cape Dutch, although he had always been under the impression that these homes were by nature single-storeyed. Dark shutters contrasted with white walls.

He didn't make a display of looking. Wouldn't show that he was impressed.

But one thing was for sure, and that was that the mattress waiting for him here would be softer than last night's.

Johnny took a turn, because the front of the house faced the mountain. He parked dead straight between two Samson-proof pillars that flanked a front door the size of a Wendy house. Was that imbuia? The Mercedes definitely wouldn't stay out here. The path led around another corner where there would have to be a garage or two or three.

Paul got out. He heard the gravel crunching under his shoes just as he got the heavy, musty smell of new wine. Good God, in this place you could get sozzled just by breathing!

The sun chose that moment for a cameo appearance. It spread its blessing over the rows and rows of vines as if it wanted to say: Look! Look! Look!

Bernard remained seated for now and it was only Johnny who got out. Who deliberately caught Paul's eye. Who went to open the boot.

Who took out something heavy, put it down, opened it up.

A wheelchair.

Johnny's look of gratification was plain to see, and Paul's ears rang with the words he'd spoken while changing the tyre: *If you had bothered to get out, Bernard, you wouldn't have to ask how I'm doing.*

Shit, faux pas deluxe.

As Johnny helped his employer out of the car, Paul considered offering additional assistance, but decided against it. Let them do it the way they always do. The chauffeur was adept, in any case, and got the man into the wheelchair as easily as he had unfolded it.

He started pushing him towards a ramp running up onto the wide stone stoep, while Paul fetched his suitcase and backpack from the boot. If only he had stood closer to the car when Johnny was putting them in, or earlier, while Johnny was taking out the spare tyre, then he would have known about the wheelchair.

He went up the six steps and caught up with the other two when the front door opened without Johnny even having rung the bell.

The portly coloured woman holding it open was wearing ordinary clothes – a mostly yellow dress with red flowers and a grey jersey of thick wool to keep the cold at bay – but her role was made apparent when she spoke. 'You're back, Mister Bernard.'

'Afternoon, Mary,' he said as he was wheeled inside.

'Did everything go well, Mister Bernard?'

No word from her for Johnny, and none for Paul either.

'Oh, it always goes well. We have a guest, so I hope you have something good in the pot for this evening.' Then, to Paul, Bernard explained: 'This is Mary, who sees to it that things run the way they should in this house … our General. And Mary, this is Paul, whatever his surname might be again.'

'Mullan. Hello, Mary.'

He held out his hand, but she just nodded. It was hard to tell how old she was, but he pegged her at forty-five. The frown lines between her thin eyebrows seemed deeper than they should have been – you don't get wrinkles that easily with a gleaming skin like hers. Apart from on your brow, if you keep frowning. It was only with the remark about her being the general that a trace of humour could be seen on her round face. What he also observed was a hint of satisfaction, and there was respect in the way she looked at Bernard.

'The guy's just staying for the night,' Johnny informed her.

'Unless it turns out differently,' Bernard said.

His voice was heavy but even, as before, though Paul could tell from his eyes that he was annoyed.

On her part, Mary made no acknowledgement of Johnny having said anything. She just wanted Paul's suitcase.

'Do you have just the one, sir? This one and the rucksack?'

'Please, I'll be fine. And call me Paul. This is all, yes.'

To their right, he saw through the open door, was a lounge just about big enough to fit one of those lock-up-and-go homes into. It was filled with objects that had stood the test of time. Antique chairs, antique carpets and antique curtains bought with old money.

'And where are the others?' asked Bernard.

'Lindsey is here somewhere.' Mary moved closer to take hold of the wheelchair as Johnny stood back. 'I think she ...'

The housekeeper looked in the direction of the footsteps. The others did too.

The girl who appeared must have been in her early twenties, Paul estimated, though she moved with the fervent energy of a teenager. Almost bouncy. She was very short, but well proportioned. Petite. Her hair couldn't really be called red; it was more of a light brown with a slight tint. She had big brown eyes and a fair skin that would have been flattered by a darker colour dress than the pastel-blue one she was wearing.

'Hello, Pops ... you tired?' She leaned over and gave Bernard a peck on the lips, then turned her head away and laughed. 'You need to go rest, but not before you introduce me to *him*.'

'I'm sure he can speak for himself.'

Paul held out his hand. 'Paul.'

'Lindsey,' she said, her hand soft in his. She looked shy suddenly, as if she wasn't convinced by her kittenish flirting either. 'Welcome to our home. Are you one of my father's—'

'He is nothing of mine. We picked him up from the side of the road.'

So that was what it sounded like when Bernard cracked a joke.

The girl smiled. Her lipstick was so faint so as to be hardly noticeable, the smattering of smoky eyeshadow equally subtle.

She had to tilt her head to be able to look Paul in the eye, as he wasn't exactly short. She didn't even come up to his shoulders.

'They had a flat tyre,' he explained, 'and I changed it.'

He saw her look obliquely at Johnny, but she didn't enquire further.

'Are we going to spend the entire afternoon in the hallway?' Bernard growled.

Immediately everyone aimed for the lounge, but they didn't get that far.

'And where is ...?' Bernard started asking.

Lindsey answered, 'I'm sure she's around here somewhere.'

Bernard interrupted himself: 'Aha.'

From her came an 'Oh.'

Because they heard footsteps, but this time not with the flightiness that had announced Lindsey's approach.

The sound came from upstairs. High heels on a wooden floor.

Like the official highway to Paradise, the staircase stretched heavenwards, and was broad enough for a number of people to walk up and down side by side. On the left was a stairlift to allow Bernard to ride up- and downstairs. At the top Paul saw a second wheelchair waiting.

Aha. The word Bernard had used. Aha, indeed. Because here it is, thought Paul.

Two feelings, or sensations, at once: the very factor he had been looking for to make today different, and the same realisation of danger he had had when he turned away from the road that could have led him to Ceres. Away from *her*.

Any road that didn't lead to her would have been the wrong one. But also the safer one. She came to a halt at the top of the stairs, all ... poise. It wasn't affectedness; it was there like the sun and the moon. Sensuality was another word that came to mind, and his body had started reacting. Her dark-brown hair was pinned up at the side in a style that seemed out of place in the Boland of today, it was one he would have expected to see in a period piece.

That was where she belonged – in one of those black-and-white films from the 40s or 50s, with tough guys and femmes fatales. If the full-colour scene they were in were to switch to black and white, it would have changed less about her than about the gathering at the base of the stairs, because her hair and eyes looked black already, her skin was already pale; from down there it looked almost as white as her blouse. Add to that the make-up, which would probably have qualified as classically dramatic, the lipstick and eyeliner both dark.

And the leather pants. How many people could wear something like those at home, in broad daylight, without looking ridiculous? Not only did they fit her shapely legs like a second skin, they might as well have been her skin. God knows how she got into them, and Paul couldn't help thinking how she would have to lie down, raising her hips, to get them off again. She stood with her leather-clad legs slightly apart.

Aha.

Her tongue swept across her lower lip lightly as she prepared to speak.

4

Mary was too quick for Paul, and now he was watching the red flowers on her dress sway along with her hips as she ascended the stairs like Hillary climbing Everest.

'It looked like Mister Bernard would like to chat,' she remarked over her shoulder, 'but if you'd prefer to rest ...?'

He made a sound.

It clearly wasn't enough, for she added a 'You look tired.'

'Rather.'

'Did you come far?'

'Rather.'

A grunt showed that Mary had got the message.

They had reached the top of the stairs. Paul's suitcase almost bumped against the wheelchair.

The passage ran in two directions, the shorter one going left, where he could see just two doors. The closest was halfway open and offered a view of a bookshelf and the corner of a wide desk. The closed door probably led to a bedroom. To the right were four closed doors, two on either side, and the door at the end of the passage was open. He could tell from the white tiles that it was a bathroom.

'This way.' Mary headed in that direction. 'Everyone sleeps upstairs. Apart from me, I sleep downstairs. Your room is to the left of the bathroom. You need to use it, yours doesn't have its own built-in bathroom.'

'En-suite,' he said automatically.

'What?' She frowned, and the grooves lay deep in her brow, like incisions.

'A built-in bathroom is an en-suite.'

'Well I told you yours doesn't have one. You need to use this one.'

'Hmm,' he answered.

She came to a halt. 'Johnny is here, across the passage from you. His room faces the mountain. He uses this bathroom too.'

'I'll try to make sure we're not in there at the same time.'

If she had noticed it was a joke, she didn't show it.

He inhaled the scent of potpourri in the bathroom as Mary opened his bedroom door with a gesture that spoke of great pride.

It was an imposing space, in reality too big for comfort, the kind of bedroom you would need to share with someone unless you wanted to feel like Gulliver in the land of giants. The brass bed was centred against a wall, the duvet large and white and fluffy. A bedside table with a lamp stood alongside. Three rugs endeavoured to cover the blonde wood floor, but there was just too much of it. A small desk with its chair pulled away took up a bit more space and a dressing table displayed an enamel jug. Built-in cupboards with shuttered doors covered the wall opposite the door, promising acres of space that were simply wasted on Paul, as he was not planning to unpack a thing.

The General stood aside. 'You still have a good two hours before dinner. You'll hear a gong, so you'll know when to come down. I'm not going to come fetch you, you'll have to listen.'

Paul suppressed a smile as he put his suitcase and backpack out of the way. Mary might intimidate most people, but her military bearing combined with her robust figure rather amused him.

'It won't be necessary to call me.'

She went out, closing the door behind her.

He locked it.

Stood there wondering why he had.

Then he shrugged. Although it was too cold to open the window, he drew back the heavy dusky-pink curtains. The shutters were open, but there was none of the phenomenal view he had expected. The oak tree that stood so close to the house even blocked the vines from sight. Judging by its size, the tree was incredibly old.

He closed the curtains. Turned around.

Two hours till dinner, Mary had said, and he needed rest, so he turned off the lights. He would have had to stumble his way to the bed if he hadn't noted its position beforehand, because the thick curtains made the room dark as night.

He lay down and got comfortable. Immediately threw one of the two pillows off the bed, because they were stuffed so thoroughly it felt as if he was sitting up. One was still too much; he liked a flat, hard pillow, yet guest houses and hotels apparently felt they would be doing you an injustice by providing one.

At home he had had the perfect pillow, one that suited the shape of his head. At night he would just lie down and that was it. In the morning he would wake up in the same position, parts of his body stiff from not moving for so long.

Now the house was gone. All the contents sold. Heaven knows where that damn pillow was.

Now he had nothing but his suitcase and a backpack and his own sorry arse.

And now you're having a little pity party, aren't you?

He exhaled slowly, but realised he wouldn't be able to fall asleep – even though the pillow was too thick, his head sank back into it as if surrounded by surprisingly sturdy clouds. It felt wrong. He listened to the silence. Granted, the room was far from the lounge, but he would have expected to hear Bernard's voice, or those of the others. Or footsteps. Or *something*. The bedroom door sealed thoroughly, thus. And it was thick too. Everything here was substantial.

Was it time to give up and turn on the light?

Later on he pressed the button on his watch and saw it was seven minutes past six.

He closed his eyes, giving weariness another chance.

He opened them and met such darkness that he wondered whether he really had done so.

Closed them again. Squeezed them shut.

And she was with him.

No, she was standing where she had been earlier, at the top of the stairs, and he was where he had been, at the bottom. They had been several metres apart, but the visual impression repeated itself with the bravura of a cleverly planned close-up shot, synchronised with dramatic strings, drums, high-contrast lighting, the works. Her lips filled the screen, her tongue swept across her lower lip as she prepared to speak.

His imagination took hold. Her tongue wasn't sweeping her lip, but his. He opened his mouth and it slid in, two tongues meeting, dancing, gliding across one another and ...

His eyes started open.

It was ...

He tried to capture the feeling. Indescribably erotic. But also disturbing. Losing control wasn't the idea, it couldn't be good. To be able to *take* control again, that was his mission. It was entirely ridiculous, fantasising about someone he wasn't even going to get to know. But at least it was harmless – his secret alone.

Good thing he'd be gone in the morning.

He closed his eyes again.

You, your right hand stretched out ahead. In it, the pistol, which moves to the rhythm of your eyes, searching the dark space.

The building, which looks fit to collapse.

Somewhere in here, danger.

Your palm, clammy against the grip. What's up with you tonight? It's not your first time in a situation like this. Far from.

A sudden loud noise very close to you, and you swing the pistol wildly, inhale sharply, the sound hard in your own ears. You'd stepped on an uneven surface. You realise it was something crunching under your shoe, maybe a piece of brick.

Get it together!

You try to control your breath, move as quietly as you can to the first open door on the left.

Someone could be waiting there, and …

And the shot rang, and it echoed, echoed again, and he cried out, feeling himself fall.

He didn't hit the ground or the floor.

It was soft, a duvet. He was on a bed.

Oh. He was *here*. He had fallen asleep after all.

The sound that had woken him was repeated. It was the gong Mary had mentioned and sounded nothing like a gunshot; there was no similarity. Just as the sound of a tyre bursting had nothing in common with pistol fire.

Nothing more was to be heard through the thick wood, but that gong you couldn't miss.

He could only hope that no one had heard him cry out, because he certainly wasn't in the mood for questioning eyes downstairs.

He realised he was panting, as in the dream. Forget it now, he thought – or as he had commanded himself back then: Get it together!

You're in the Boland, he reminded himself, and all's well. You're just about to have a meal and get back some of your strength, you're going to listen to an old man prattling, you're going to forget your own stuff for a while and see the kind of life other people lead.

Life … A few times over the last months, when he'd get to a bridge and watch the muddied white water churn far below, or even more enticing, a deep ravine with teeth of stone ready to cut and smash, he'd been keen to jump. His soul had died that night, hadn't it? How could you keep believing in salvation when it never came?

Yet each time he had continued walking.

He swung his legs from the bed, but remained sitting for a while. He felt for the table, found it, felt for the cord, found it and followed it, found the switch and turned on the light.

Something ran across his hand. He shuddered, went cold from head to toe.

Instinctively he wanted to crush the spider with his other hand, but stopped himself just in time when he realised it was the harmless kind; it didn't *have* to die. He shook it off onto the bedside table, where it scurried away to safety, back into the dark.

5

There really were still people who ate by candlelight. And not for financial reasons, or because of Eskom.

There was no display of majesty and status, only style and class. Bernard sat at the head of the ten-seater table. He was dressed comfortably. To Paul, his jacket looked as if it might have been bought at Edgars or any other department store, but he realised he had an untrained eye and that it surely came from a shop where you practically had to pay just to look at the display.

Lindsey was seated on Bernard's left.

And *she* was on his right.

Michelle.

Next to Michelle, Johnny. Still in his chauffeur's uniform, which seemed unnecessary at this time of day, but there you had it.

And opposite Johnny, next to Lindsey, him. The guest.

Diagonally opposite, Paul watched her mouth. He had always liked the name Michelle. *Michelle, ma belle, these are words that go together well* ... He watched La Belle Michelle take a bite of chicken from her fork. Even her chewing was sensual. And sophisticated. He watched her swallow, watched the movement of her throat. A slender neck that led the eye to the deceptively simple dress of navy blue, the neckline not too low, but her arms bare, as if she were immune to the cold.

She could be scarcely five years older than Lindsey, had maybe just crossed the thirty mark, but she seemed to have a lifetime more of experience.

Lindsey.

She had turned towards him, head tilted, and he realised she had spoken.

'Sorry, I didn't hear that.'

'I asked where you were going.' She smiled. She smiled a lot, and it lit up her face. He wondered whether she was nervous, whether that was why her hands fluttered so. She reminded him of a wagtail, her skinny legs being in almost perpetual motion. She was wearing a different dress from the one she'd had on that afternoon. Another pastel, this time a soft pink, and he didn't think he was flattering himself in his suspicion that she had deliberately chosen it with him in mind.

'I'm not sure yet.'

Always give the safest answer. If you were to say you don't know, or that it hardly makes a difference, the questions would really start.

'That's interesting ...'

From across the table came a sniff that was meant to imply that nothing about Paul could possibly interest Johnny. Few people could match him in the ability to state his case without saying a word.

It hadn't passed Bernard by. He was observant, just as Paul was observant – and Paul observed that this employer was not pleased with his employee being so transparent regarding his guest.

No unpleasantness now, thought Paul. Johnny could be castigated tomorrow, if necessary.

But when Bernard spoke, it wasn't to the chauffeur. 'Michelle?'

'Hmm?'

'The salt.'

God, the way she handed it to him. Even the way she picked up the salt-shaker and the soft sweep of her arm before she handed it over made him hornier than he had been in ages. Surely he was imagining things. Surely she couldn't possess all the characteristics to which he was reacting. Maybe she was as thick as a plank and just lucky enough not to appear that way. And as for sensuality, maybe all her previous lovers could vouch for how lame she had turned out to be in the sack.

That was something the man at the head of the table would be able to tell him more about. Though the two women looked nothing alike, upon first seeing them, Paul had assumed that Michelle and Lindsey were sisters. In fact, the woman on the other side of the table had a vastly different role in this house.

Bernard gave his food a thorough sprinkling of salt.

'Pops, maybe take it easy with the salt,' Lindsey said. 'It's bad for the kidneys.'

Bernard's mouth twitched.

Knowing his eyes were about to wander Michelle's way again, Paul searched for something else to think about. Like how quiet the house was. The only discernible sounds were the ones they were making at table.

The house had every luxury, but for one obvious item – there might have been TVs in some of the bedrooms, but Paul had not yet noticed any downstairs. It was refreshing. In none of his recent abodes had he been able to escape the goggle-box. Time and time again he found himself turning the thing on anew, only to be confronted with the three eternal truths once more:

1) Local content was safe and predictable, as if entirely produced by the same two or three small production houses, which likely belonged to chums of the station managers. A blend of conservative and common seemed to remain the Holy Grail.

2) Reality shows were becoming ever more out of touch with any normal person's concept of reality, with 'stars' who had to keep giving up more privacy and dignity than previous participants to justify their place on the programmes and were starting to make the Kardashians look like the epitome of good taste.

3) In a country that remained as race-conscious as ever, people still defined and boxed themselves in with the same old rhetoric gleaned from the mouths of party leaders, although the way they talked about it you'd think they had dreamed it up themselves.

TV, you will not be missed ...

Paul's attention returned to the people around the table. He watched Bernard dig into the food Mary had prepared. She was the only absent member of the household, presumably being in the kitchen; there were no other staff as far as Paul could tell. The food – which needed no seasoning – could have been made by a team of people each focusing on a specific dish: chicken so tender it fell off the bone, peas fresh explosions of flavour, creamy sweet potato.

Lindsey tilted her head again. 'Paul, if you don't know where you're going, you can at least tell us where you've come from!'

She didn't have much tact, he thought. But she was young and had time to acquire it. It would arrive along with sophistication, and then she'd lose the naïveté of her smile and the fluttering motions of her fingers.

'Pretoria.'

'Had you had enough of Pretoria?'

'Yes.'

He hadn't meant to sound so blunt. He picked up his wine glass. The red was soft on the palate, and though he was no expert, in his opinion he was tasting quality. The bottle was turned with the label facing away from him, but he didn't believe it was from this farm. Someone would have said if it was.

'And—'

Bernard interrupted her with the demeanour of someone used to stepping in. 'Lindsey, it seems to me our guest knows that the less you say, the less you give away.'

Everyone laughed politely. Lindsey's decision to swallow her next question was so obvious she might as well have held up a sign to announce it. Whereas any other daughter might have been annoyed at such an admonishment, she simply blushed lightly and smiled at the head of the table. Paul knew by now it was a habit of hers to tilt her head when she looked at someone; it might have come about because she needed to look up so often.

She continued eating.

Bernard did too, with big elbow movements. It was the greatest irony that, out of them all, he was the one in a wheelchair, because his sentences were mostly punctuated with grand gestures, the sort that belonged to the kind of person who dominates meetings and strides around seated parties.

And this felt fairly similar to being at a meeting, when he sat making remarks that sounded more like announcements.

Michelle looked up and her eyes met Paul's.

Don't give anything away, he thought. She was just another person at this table. He had to keep it that way.

Again he thought of those old black-and-white movies as he looked at the navy-blue dress against her fair skin. What was that style called again? Film noir. Movies that often had more to say than the studio darlings did, despite miserly budgets and the typical and therefore predictable ingredients. The hero, fallible and swept along by events. The brutal nature of such events. The fatal decisions made. The lighting casting shadows that so effectively signified ever-present evil. And, to crown it all, the femme fatale, a deadly woman whose head would be full of ideas leading inexorably to a terrible outcome.

'So, do you just live out of the one suitcase?'

The voice of the deadly woman diagonally opposite him was

slightly husky. It showed interest, that was all. The playfulness he wanted to hear wasn't really there.

'Well, there's a backpack too.'

That's it. Keep it light. It was good to have an excuse to pay attention to her the way he had been wanting to all along. His damned eyes wouldn't leave her in peace, so he dared not look at her, or in any case not for long. Bernard would notice, and Johnny too. Lindsey might not have noticed, but they were men. They would be able to tell instantly from the way he was looking at her that his thoughts were filled with the things a man would like to do to a woman like that.

A corner of her mouth twitched. 'Suitcase and backpack, then.'

Bernard cleared his throat. 'Michelle, it looks like you have a short memory. You'll remember that you also arrived here with just a suitcase ... and look at your wardrobe now!'

So there it was. Paul realised he'd had reason for concern. Bernard had found her too friendly and put her in her place.

And that's how she accepted it. Or seemingly so. She looked at Bernard and then back down at her plate. Carried on eating.

Was he imagining things, or was the girl in the pink dress next to him suppressing a smile?

And Johnny, was he on the brink of frowning? Maybe the man had virtues like warmth and empathy after all. Or, more likely, Michelle had the same effect on him. Or was it that he, a fellow underling, was sensitive to that kind of remark?

It became evident soon enough that the near-frown had been observed too.

'Johnny ... talking about clothes ...'

'What is it, Bernard?' He spoke with caution.

'Or, no, let's have dessert first. I assume there is dessert?'

'Oh, most certainly, Mister Bernard.'

Mary was at the swing door that led to the kitchen. Despite usually being observant, Paul had not noticed her enter this time. She disappeared from view and reappeared with a trolley. She wheeled it over to Bernard, took his plate and started rounding up the other crockery. She was filled with silent power, like a statue come to life. Without her noticing, Paul studied the round face of which the parts – wide mouth, flattish nose, deep-set eyes – seemed somewhat unfinished, as if shaped by a sculptor with plenty of clay but little patience. He could again discern the force of her loyalty towards Bernard, and her care for Lindsey, but there seemed to be precious little for the rest of them.

The pudding arrived, small, but rich and filling. Paul couldn't remember ever having eaten a more delicious crème brûlée.

Done with his dinner, Bernard placed his teaspoon on the plate. It was a sign that he wanted to say something, though with anyone else it would simply have been a case of them setting down their cutlery.

'Paul ... seeing as you still haven't decided where you're going, you can't be in too much of a hurry to get there.'

'I'm not.' He was curious as to what Bernard was aiming at.

'Can you drive?'

'Yes.'

'And you have a licence?'

'Yes.'

'Then we're in a position to help each other. I'm looking for a chauffeur.'

Dead silence.

Broken by a dismayed voice. 'But ...'

'Don't you worry, Johnny. I'm not planning to get rid of you yet. Paul, what do you say?'

'It's ...' he gave his host a sideways glance, 'a little unexpected.'

'It's not hard work. I don't go out much. Really only when I need to be in town, or sometimes for a meal somewhere. As for the uniform, I would say you and Johnny are the same size. Johnny, you can just give him yours.'

Paul frowned. 'I—'

'You don't have to be concerned that I won't pay you a decent wage.'

He nearly laughed. 'No, it's not that.'

'You'll have to do something to earn money, unless you're wealthier than you look. And you have to lay your head down somewhere. It might as well be here.'

All very logical.

Johnny had regained some control. 'Bernard, we don't know him.' He looked at Paul. 'Sorry, but we know nothing about you.'

'Thank you for your concern, Johnny.' By lowering his pitch, the older man made it very clear how little he appreciated it. 'But we didn't know that much about you when you started with us either.' He pointed in Mary's direction. 'She needs a helper. She carries a heavy load, as you know. This is the solution. You'll assist her from now on. So, Paul ...'

Sometimes you get moments like that. Not the sort you'd be surprised to remember. The kind that you would remember because they were about to make things change, although you didn't know how; you only knew you'd made it to a door and needed to choose whether to open it or leave it closed.

Johnny was part of the moment, with a face that showed Paul he wanted to protest but wouldn't dare.

As was Mary, who, as she cleared the dessert plates, took delight in Johnny's consternation, but without any outward display of emotion. Mary, who, for a change, was not frowning.

Lindsey, who didn't try to hide she was hoping that Paul would agree.

And Lord knows he wanted to. Because the day hadn't taken the same turn as all the rest, after all. Yet there was the feeling, and this he would have to take into account, that he was being dragged into something. Slowly still, at the moment, but it had started. Yet what was that something? There were two parts to it: he knew for sure that his long search had delivered him to Journey's End so that he could find an answer, and that it was connected to the premonition he'd had. Maybe it was time to start taking the possibility of a sixth sense seriously.

His seemed to be screaming at him that there was no happy ending waiting here. That he would be taking the first step on a road that could lead to nothing but disaster.

Not too late to say no.

He looked in her direction as discreetly as possible.

And she narrowed her eyes just a fraction, moved her head just enough for the others not to notice she was nodding.

6

Paul was just about to close his bedroom door – and lock it, because that came naturally – when someone pushed it open. Mary stepped inside, the smell of fresh-cut flowers drifting in with her.

She deposited a small vase with white roses on the desk, stepped back, repositioned it and was visibly pleased. She looked around as if taking stock of how much damage had been done here already, frown at full strength. Then she held out the blanket that she had been holding under her left arm.

Paul tried a smile. 'And the flowers?'

'The rooms always get it.'

'So, now that I'm staying longer than one night, I get roses and a blanket?'

Her reply was businesslike. 'You can get the uniforms from Johnny tomorrow. There are three of them, so—'

'One to wear, one in the wash and one spare.'

'You'll have to wear it all the time, like him. Do you have decent black shoes?' She looked at his feet disapprovingly. 'Or will we have to buy you some?'

'I have a pair.'

'That's good. Because we don't know how long you'll be here.'

Paul wanted to laugh. As if Bernard Russell couldn't afford to buy someone a pair of shoes!

'You're taking quite a chance by just letting someone in here.'

'Mister Bernard has good instincts.' She seemed ever so slightly obliging now that he had acknowledged that she was justified in having reservations. 'And if he decides something then he does it. You've seen for yourself now. And he likes taking chances.' Something stirred behind her eyes, it seemed she was in doubt whether to mention it, but then she pointed out, 'But someone else took too *many* chances ...'

'Johnny?' he encouraged, when it appeared she wanted to close the subject.

'Someone who gave too much attention to someone *else* ...'

'Ah.'

He wondered whether perhaps she meant Michelle rather than Johnny. He recalled the way Bernard had humiliated her at table.

It had nothing to do with him. He had to ensure it stayed that way.

Mary got back to business. 'You need to make your own bed in the morning. I'm not the maid. Same way Johnny has to make his.'

Lower in rank than Johnny you couldn't get in this house, it seemed.

'I assumed I'd be doing it myself.'

'Well, goodnight then.'

He was closing the door behind her when he heard a sound. Not Mary walking away, but something on the stairs. Then came Mary's voice, a soft greeting.

Curiosity took over. He had almost forgotten the feeling, the drive for knowledge to which you're not always entitled. Hastily he turned out the light so that he wouldn't be seen. Opened the door a crack and waited.

There was a humming sound. That would be Bernard's stairlift, he realised.

And it was. Yet it was Michelle who first came into view: her head, her neckline, the navy blue of her dress. Then Bernard glided into the picture. She kept up with him.

Paul started wondering how obvious his open door really was, but he knew that was because he believed she should be able to sense him standing here. A force like the one he felt couldn't just stream forth and dissolve in the atmosphere.

If she had noticed anything, she didn't let it show. He watched her helping Bernard out of the stairlift and into the wheelchair ... or rather how she wanted to and how he pushed her hands away, although not with the brusqueness of earlier. And then, struggling, he did it by himself.

Michelle still took hold of the handles and started pushing the wheelchair to the left. Which meant that room was theirs.

Then.

She turned her head. Looked in Paul's direction.

It was an effort not to quickly shut the door.

Was she smiling?

He took a step back. He felt like a peeping Tom caught in the act, but sound logic told him she couldn't have seen him.

But.

He knew she knew.

He heard a crack, the groan of hinges, and took another peep, in time to see her pushing the wheelchair into their bedroom.

Now the question was how it all worked once that door closed at night.

7

Bernard was already lying on his side of the bed, closest to the wardrobe. Michelle was still in the en-suite bathroom, door ajar, allowing him to hear the goings on: a spritz of something here, the rush of water there. More than once he caught flashes of black and white through the gap.

The black of her lingerie, the rosy pink of her body, white in the bright light.

It was the kind of enviable body usually sculpted by athletics or hours in the gym, even in the case of younger women.

Good genes? Bernard had no idea; she wasn't one to talk about her family. Her entire past was a closed book. He preferred it that way. He'd have been able to find out if he'd wanted, but like this he had been able to make her a creation of his own imagining. Once you knew certain things, they were impossible to forget. What was more, although she might have been holding back plenty, she was most generous in other instances. Such as now, because she knew only too well how he watched her getting ready. She *gave* him those glimpses, the small reveals part and parcel of her evening bathroom ritual.

And then she was done. She opened the door and turned off the light behind her. Smelt good. She had so many lotions and potions.

Bernard's voice rasped. 'Come here.'

Michelle looked at him as if she was only becoming aware of him now.

'What do you say?'

Her tone was nuanced. Playful. Strict. Cool.

'I suppose one says please,' he answered.

'If you know what to say, say it.'

It was a game of power, of course, what else? But win or lose, it made no difference. He took her in, her dark hair matching her lingerie so well, and in that moment nothing else mattered. He was nearly beside himself with arousal. Plenty of women would have been able to get him that far, but not time and time again as if by a magic switch. Not always knowing her thoughts, at least most of the time, made it more intense. Knowing that she wouldn't have stuck around had he been a pauper added something extra.

'Please,' he said.

Strange how hoarse his voice always became.

'Please who?'

Hers was husky. It was naturally that way, but she often exaggerated it because she knew he liked it.

'Please, Michelle.'

'You were very mean to me out there, in front of everyone.' She came closer and he tried to touch her, but her firm thigh escaped his fingers by a few centimetres. 'I'm not convinced you're sorry enough.'

'I am sorry enough.' It had to show on his face, because dammit, he *was*. Why did he have to be so nasty to her? Damn his insecurity!

Her hands reached for her bra clasp.

'Is mean old Bernard going to try that again?'

'No, Bernard won't.'

She showed him mercy and moved within reach. Now his eager

hands would explore her thighs and stomach. And her breasts, because the bra was undone; it fell away to expose them.

'We both know Bernard is always Bernard.'

But she stood there, acquiescent, allowing him to keep touching, now with just the one hand on her breast, the nipple squeezed between his thumb and index finger. Because beneath the duvet his other hand was in his lap. He might have lost the use of his legs, but not all departments had been closed.

She was still holding the bra. She moved aside, leaving his hand clutching the air. She waved the scrap of black lace in his face, laughed.

He snapped at it like a dog.

Then she was back in his reach and he staked his claim with the free hand. She came closer, leaned over him, and he pressed his head against her. Her face he couldn't see anymore. Was she looking down at his thinning crown, now that he was sucking the nipple, or was she staring at the wardrobe door, void of expression?

She made an encouraging sound.

It wasn't important what she looked like now. He didn't want to know. He might see her eyes betray a not quite acceptable emotion.

Her body, *that* remained his.

8

Paul had fallen asleep. Despite not being entirely at ease, his tiredness had helped.

And as expected, the mattress was a significant improvement on that of the night before, and on those of the last several weeks.

The silence of the room.

The wine with dinner.

The knowledge that he was off the road for the time being, whatever might happen in this place.

Nevertheless, sleeping was not the same thing as getting rest. His clammy brow and the twitching beneath his eyelids attested to this fact.

You enter the house, your right hand stretched out in front of you. Gripping the pistol. Moonlight through broken windows.

There is something about the building, otherworldly. You would have thought it haunted had you believed in that sort of thing.

You try, but the sense of a threat won't be reasoned away. Knowing there is no such thing as ghosts just makes it worse – the danger is real and physical.

The pistol is all you have to defend yourself against it. But the barrel can point in only one direction at a time. The butt is slippery in your palm.

What's happening? You should be used to this kind of situation! You were before.

In the passage. Then there's a loud crunch close by, and you swing the pistol. Your breath rasps. You realise you stepped on something, probably a piece of rubble, chastise yourself, get it together, steady your breath. Gingerly, you force yourself towards the first door to the left, a deep, black hole in which someone might be waiting for you. You've been making enough of a racket for him to be ready for you.

What you're not seeing – what you'll only realise later – is the person around the corner, a bit further away. The one who had discerned your approach and retreated quietly.

You're going to be such an easy target.

His eyes sprung open. Surrounding him was nothing but darkness, and the fear dissolved almost instantly. There was no danger here, or in any case, none immediate.

Silence.

He was always glad when he started awake at this point: by no means happy about the nightmare returning yet again, but for being spared the full version.

He had opened the window a crack and left a gap in the curtains before he settled in for the night, so that he could at least hear the sounds of the night outside, doubtless twigs and leaves brushing against each other. And especially now that his eyes had adjusted it was no longer so dark.

He stifled a yawn, found himself drowsy again after all, despite the upset ...

Yet things were not in order – he whipped his head around to face the door. The handle turned.

The door was pushed open.

Momentarily he was petrified, unable to move. It was a miracle he hadn't pissed himself, or maybe he had. He couldn't be sure. It was just like *that* time, when everything had just stopped working, apart from his racing breath.

There was a figure entering the room.

Just a figure, before his brain received the message that it was wearing a white nightdress, that it was her.

She closed the door quietly and started towards the bed, her movements supremely feminine.

'If you don't want to come to me, I'll just have to come to you.'

Somehow he managed to get up, make it to her, grab hold of her. They fell down onto the bed and his breath sped up again.

But there he lay alone, she was gone, had never been there. He turned his head to check, looking towards the closed door. Which he had locked. She would never have been able to get in.

At least it hadn't been the bad-house dream again. Since that night it had been coming almost non-stop.

He heard an owl hooting.

9

The land baron and ruler of many lay swept away in dreams. An orgasm will trump the best sleeping tablet.

Bernard Russell, entrepreneur, decision-maker.

And snorer.

When he lay on his side, he didn't snore. But people paralysed from the waist down seldom lie that way. It sounded as if his lungs were tearing up, and it was incredible that it didn't wake him.

Despite the darkness Michelle could visualise all the costly items around her. That was how well she knew the position of each. It could remain pitch dark and someone could turn her around and give her just one point of reference and she would be able to navigate the bedroom collision-free. She had full usufruct of all these things, which was either progress in life or a celebration of her disgrace; it depended on her frame of mind on a given day.

She was sitting on the armrest of a throne or lying in a ditch she had dug herself.

Outside, an owl hooted.

She turned onto her side, towards Bernard, and beheld his sleeping profile, the open mouth allowing the rasping to be brought forth unhindered and with gusto. Even in the dark and with nobody to observe her, her eyes showed nothing, as she had taught herself.

But they saw everything.

DAY 2

10

The roosters of the district, each king of his own castle, announced the morning before everyone was quite ready to acknowledge it. That today would be less rainy than yesterday was already apparent as the sun slowly rose from behind the mountains and Riebeek-Kasteel started lightening up. There was still a chill in the air, but the clouds above the mist were fine as a spider's web, and the dew would soon be dispelled by the sunlight.

Those creatures that could do so clung to the spots they had chosen to spend the night.

Riebeek-Kasteel was quiet, cars still in their places of overnight rest. Blinds were drawn, windows were closed and shop doors locked, including those of the trendy tourist-focused outlets near the church. A dog sauntered across the road without stopping to look left or right, but had never been in less danger of being run over.

Further off, in the direction of Journey's End, the mist remained so dense the world seemed to end right there. But beyond the haze there was indeed life.

Johnny's reflection took faint shape at the slightly open window where he was frowning and exhaling smoke into the cold air. He was in regular clothes. Behind him, his bed was neatly made.

Lindsey was freshly showered and drying her hair. She had it tumbling forward; in high school a friend had told her this method boosted volume, and wasn't that the truth! She stepped on one of the fluffy toys on the floor. They were on display elsewhere in the room too: teddies, a couple of little pigs, a lion, a zebra, an elephant.

Mary, meanwhile, was wiping down the stove. It was old-school, tough, made to last. She hardly ever used the microwave. On the counter a packet of bacon lay alongside a bowl of eggs laid by her own hens.

11

The mist was lifting. Each time Paul looked out of his window, things were greener; there were more outlines. They emerged like photographs developed the old-fashioned way, paper placed in the right series of solutions, allowing images to take shape gradually.

To see beyond the oak, though, he had to position himself carefully. The grand old tree would come into its own in summer, when it most likely got as hot as hell in the valley.

He had on the same clothes as the day before. It had taken just a week on the road to lose the compulsion to wear a clean set every day – that would just have meant more items that would need to be washed somewhere. He'd got used to soaping and rinsing shirts, underwear and socks and leaving them on a heating pipe to dry overnight – if the room contained something of that nature.

This one didn't.

But his clothes could be washed here. He would be staying here, after all, even though it was still difficult to get used to the idea.

He looked over his shoulder, at his bed, which was still as untidy as when he had woken up. Rarely had a bed asserted so loudly that someone had had a restless night. He wanted to neaten it up, but it felt like too much effort for something that was unnecessary. It was his room now, which meant it was no one else's business what it looked like in here.

Knock-knock at the door.

'Come in.' When the handle turned without the door opening, he realised he must have locked it again after returning from the bathroom.

'Sorry, I'm coming.' He went to open up. 'Oh. Morning.'

'Here are your things.' This was Johnny's version of a greeting. It was strange to see him in everyday clothes, a black polo-neck and black jeans: in the dark all he would have needed to add was a balaclava to vanish into thin air. He walked past Paul with a folded grey uniform in each hand and placed them on the duvet. 'If they don't get lost in this bloody disaster zone.'

'Thank you.'

Without another word, Johnny walked past him, accompanied by the scent of tobacco. It was on his breath too. This wasn't true of all cigarettes, but there were a handful of brands that fouled up the smoker's breath royally and in this case Paul's guess was Chesterfield. He shrugged when the door closed behind the sour bugger.

Then he took off his clothes and started dressing for the new job. Who would have thought he'd ever be trying out this line of work? As Bernard had predicted, the uniform fitted well, but the jacket was marginally too tight around the shoulders. The white shirt was his own. The reflection he saw in the mirror was more convincing than he had expected: the drifter turned chauffeur.

Even so, he did not feel comfortable on his way down the long, wide staircase. He was self-conscious, and the feeling would probably remain until everyone had at least seen him in this outfit. The slight straining across his shoulders was a constant reminder that this was a role he would be filling only temporarily.

It was already after eight, but it didn't sound as if much was going on in the house. On the top floor, all the doors except for the one into what was clearly the study had been closed. What time did these people have their breakfast?

He found Lindsey in the dining room with half a fried egg left on her plate. Her face broke into a smile.

'Good morning, Paul! I hope you got some sleep.'

'Hi. I didn't know what time you get up here.' He pulled up the chair across from hers.

'You could have slept in a bit!'

It was a good thing she wore so little make-up, because it made her smooth complexion come into its own.

'When I'm up, I'm up.'

'As long as you aren't all ready and set on my father's behalf. He doesn't get up till reeeeeeally late. He and ...'

Lindsey went quiet. Her smile was gone.

Last night he hadn't been able to determine what she thought about Michelle, but this gave him an indication. Most girls would find it difficult if their fathers had a lover barely older than they were themselves.

She smiled again. 'Mary will bring your breakfast in a moment.'

But it was Johnny who came out of the kitchen seconds later with a plate of bacon, two fried eggs, half a fried tomato and a slice of bread, which he placed in front of Paul.

Bam.

'Thank you.' Paul heard the discomfort breaking through his voice.

No answer. Johnny just pointed at the silver pot between Paul and Lindsey to indicate he could help himself to coffee.

'I see,' said Paul.

No answer. Johnny left.

Paul started on his breakfast. It must have been the fresh air, as he was ravenous.

Lindsey leaned forward and whispered, 'You don't need to feel bad about Johnny. That's just the way my father is. He doesn't mean it that way.'

He swallowed before speaking. 'Doesn't mean it how?'

'Oh ...' She changed tack. 'The silence must be strange for you. I mean, after Pretoria. That's where you said you were from?'

'I left Pretoria quite some time ago. There might be some things I miss, but the noise isn't one of them.'

He could see Lindsey was dying to ask *what* he missed. He had always been able to tell when a girl was interested in him. And who knew, another time, another place, if he hadn't had so much to deal with, and if she hadn't been in the same house as someone who made him oblivious to any other woman ... *then* maybe.

She sighed. 'Well, I miss Cape Town.' When she saw he didn't understand, she said, 'That's where we were living until about a year ago.'

'Oh? I assumed you'd been here all along.'

It had appeared to Paul that Bernard Russell and this place were well intertwined, and that took time.

'No, only since my father got the urge to downsize. Did you think he was a farmer?'

'Isn't he?'

'No!' Lindsey laughed. 'Not in the least. He has people that take care of those things for him. Everything here.'

'What is his line of business then?'

She hesitated. 'There's a question for you.'

'Oh yes?'

The hesitation passed. She was in the mood for conversation. 'Anything. He is ... a middleman. Someone wants to sell something, someone wants to buy it, and he brings them together. He has connections everywhere. And now you know as much as I know!' She lifted her cup and took a sip of coffee that must have gone cold. 'I don't ask anymore.'

'I always ask too much. Old habits.' Her open-heartedness was infectious and made Paul add, 'I was a policeman.'

'Oh. Really? And ...'

'And you? What are you going to be doing?'

Her big brown eyes went wide. 'What do you mean, what am I going to be doing?'

'With your life. Study, work ...'

He discovered that he really wanted to know. It came as a surprise, because he had been so caught up in his own private little bit of hell that it had been a while since he was bothered with what anyone else was doing.

'I finished school and then ... and then nothing.' For a moment, the yearning for a thousand undefined pleasures and challenges was written over Lindsey's face. And then the smile returned. 'But it's lovely here. And I'm not bored. And my father didn't want me to ...'

Daddy's girl, he thought. If your father doesn't want you to do anything, you won't. No issue.

'Do you have a boyfriend?'

Once it was out, he knew it was the wrong question – she might view it as encouragement. Why did his tongue sometimes have such a mind of its own?

She laughed, perhaps feeling a little awkward. 'I'm not about to become a farmer's wife. Anyway, any guy ... after my father, you know ...' There was a little frown, but then the smile was back again. 'How can a man fill shoes like those?'

Indeed. Paul didn't answer, just thought about how many girls were hoping for a man just like their father, and how that search became much more complicated when he was someone like Bernard Russell.

Lindsey stayed seated while he finished eating.

You might think you're after a man like *me* this time, he thought. But if you'd like to save yourself great misery, find yourself someone completely different.

He had never been a good person. Had never been under that illusion. Born into sin, and from the time he was capable of thought, never shied away from ideas of the wrong kind; it was a part of himself as much as were his hands and feet. Desires, urges, wishes, hate. Sometimes they all felt the same.

There was the classmate in Grade Eight he had beaten up so severely that the boy – what was his name again? – ended up with his jaw hanging from his face like a broken hinge and lost the sight in one eye. He simply couldn't remember what led to it, really he couldn't, even though the adults had believed he was lying. He just knew the guy was looking for it, or that's how it had felt. There could have been no real reason to go overboard like that, and he had since come to realise that it had been something trivial that he had wanted to regard as important at that moment, just so he could have a fight about it.

A few years later there was Lizzy, his sort-of girlfriend who he got drunk just so that he could screw her, after he found out she had gone to the movies with another guy. Although he had lost interest in her by that time and had his eye on a different girl, it wasn't part of the plan for her to go grazing in other pastures before he did. She'd got pregnant, he'd heard several months later, but he told himself it was the other guy's baby. By that stage he was already at reform school, which offered far more opportunities for violence. Paul Mullan was destined for ruin. He could read the damning judgement on every adult face.

One day he at last found himself sufficiently concerned by his behaviour to want to see if there was something he could do about it. Not to suddenly change into a nice guy; he would feel like the biggest phoney on the planet if he tried to do that, but he had to start thinking about a career. He had to do *something* in the world of grown-ups. He decided his childhood was over, the time he could have been irresponsible and allowed all the bad out. The time during which he'd lost so much. Like his father who had declared him a write-off early on, and his mother who eventually was forced to agree. His pals had always been few and far between, moving on to find less volatile friendships. As for family members who wanted nothing to do with him, there was no shortage of those. He couldn't wipe away the past, would never forget what he had done, and certainly couldn't expect anyone else to.

His rage wasn't spent, far from it, but he would no longer be able to use his youth as an excuse, not even to himself. It was only logical that that phase would come to an end at the time of his matric finals. What would follow was either the ruin so many had predicted, or …

So he did it. Channelled it. Good thing he had realised there was a way out – that certain forms of violence are sanctioned. The right kind of man of violence was needed to keep the other kind from doing damage to good people.

There was a bonus. Whenever he held his pistol, it was as if his dick became a metre long. But that wasn't the most important thing. Each perpetrator he caught was like preventing himself from doing something wrong. It felt natural. He was doing the right thing without feeling he was living a lie or trying to pull the wool over anyone's eyes, himself included. Sometimes he liked to think that was how most people functioned. And if you were in the police, violence and other irregularities were part of the job and there was no need to feel ashamed about it. He could believe in it.

Hallelujah.

But he should have known it was too simple. That his real punishment still lay ahead, because his time in the reformatory hadn't been enough of a penance. *More* was required.

And now? Today he had a hole inside where for so many years there had been something with which he could justify all those wrongful thoughts and deeds. A part of him that had, perversely, offered the absolution that he now had to do without. He had even wondered whether he might revert to what he once had been, but no, he didn't think so – nothing could grow in such a void, not even evil.

He was a joke. Took fright at the tiniest thing. The kind of pathetic loser he would once have laughed at before he took his fists to him.

'You don't have to, you can leave it just like that,' Lindsey tried to stop him when he picked up his plate and hers, but he took them through to the kitchen anyway.

'You didn't need to bring them through,' Johnny said too. 'Just put them down over there.' He continued wiping the counter.

'Where's Mary?' Paul asked.

'Not here right now.'

Wipe, wipe.

'So can we talk?'

'You can talk; I don't know what you want *me* to say.'

But the wiping stopped.

If you knew what I once was, Paul thought, you'd be more careful. In those days I would have ...

Keep it together, he ordered himself. The way you were is nothing to be proud of. And even if you hate the way you feel these days, and the way you view yourself, you're probably still a better person.

'Listen, pal, it wasn't my idea to take your job. And I want to let you know you'll get it back soon, ten to one.'

'How would that be, *pal*?'

Yes, Chesterfield most likely. The first captain under whose command Paul had worked in the police was a thirty-a-day man, always with that pack in hand, and his breath had had exactly the same reek.

'Your boss and I, we have no contract. He hasn't even told me what he's planning to pay me. I'm only around out of curiosity.'

'Oh, you're trying him out, not the other way around?'

The guy really was asking for it. But in a world where so many people skirt around the issue and pretend they're something other than they really are, it was quite refreshing to come across someone who showed how he felt about you.

Just rather too well.

'If this place doesn't agree with me, I'm out of here. That's how it works.'

'That your life philosophy? And what am I supposed to do with that?'

'Whatever you want.' He was starting to enjoy the feeling of Johnny trying to provoke him without him giving the desired response. 'You can file it wherever you like.'

Nice stroke, that one, but he wouldn't show it. And Johnny had felt it, because his voice was a little pinched when he spoke again. 'Here's some free advice ...'

'Free usually means worthless.'

'You just watch out for Michelle.'

Paul realised he had let his surprise show, but that was no crisis. The guy had likely just picked up his interest in her because he was interested himself.

'Seems to me if *you* had been a little more cautious, you would still have been driving that Merc. And I'm not after her.'

'Oh, not?' The way those teeny eyes narrowed even further showed he had seen through Paul. 'Are you a bloody fag then?'

'Why, would you be interested?'

Johnny let a laugh slip through. 'Okay, then ... but some women are bad news for any man. You still think you're in control ...'

He let go of the kitchen cloth and slowly dragged a nicotine-stained finger across his throat.

12

Everything the ads said about Mercedes was true. The engine purred, the wheels sang and the seat felt as if it had been designed especially for your very own backside.

After breakfast he had come to sit behind the wheel of this piece of German luxury to get used to the sensation, and by now they were old friends. He assumed it was the most recent model, because Bernard Russell might well favour a house chock full of antiques, but only the very latest model would do when it came to a set of wheels.

'Tell him to get on it, we've lost enough time already. And if he isn't up to it, someone else will be.'

The deep voice droned from the back seat. That cell phone would also be the very latest; Bernard carried it around like a paperback, while Paul had had his for years and it was small enough to slip into his pocket.

He closed his ears to the rest of the conversation as there were plenty of other things to focus on. Like the surroundings, with mountains in the blue yonder, shaped like the lines on a graph, lilac and mauve under the startling cerulean sky. Like the fact that when he got into this car yesterday, he would have laughed if someone had told him he'd be driving it today.

Like the fact that she was sitting diagonally behind him.

He saw her reflection in the rear-view mirror when they turned off the dirt road onto the tar. She was looking through the window, her slim neck on display. Her hair was down. Dark eyeliner, dark red lips, blusher, a maroon dress with high collar. No jewellery, although he was certain she had enough of the stuff.

He was aware of her perfume, too: subtle, but unmissable nevertheless. Sweet, but not cloying. He couldn't exactly distinguish between the various kinds of perfume, but he knew this one was the kind that came in small bottles that would take a generous chunk out of most men's monthly salary.

His eyes were drawn to the mirror again, where they met hers, and he quickly looked back to the road. His neck seemed to be glowing, although Bernard was still in fiery conversation and therefore shouldn't have noticed anything that could raise suspicion.

'Let me know.' Bernard cut off the call and continued, as if it was part of the same conversation, 'When last were you behind the wheel of a car?'

'Why? Is my driving that bad?' asked Paul.

'Interesting manner you have.'

'And that would be?'

'Not answering questions. But I'll get your story out of you yet.'

Paul allowed the amusement to show in his voice. 'It's probably not as gripping as you think.'

Irony is more effective than rudeness if you want to keep someone at a distance. It can only work if the person has a measure of intelligence, but no one could accuse this man of a lack thereof.

'Oh, I doubt that very much,' answered Bernard. 'What do you think, Michelle?'

In the mirror Paul saw her turn her head. She smiled lightly. 'I have no opinion.'

Bernard laughed, a rather jagged sound. 'Would be a darn first, a woman with no opinion!'

An utmost display of power, thought Paul. Most bullying behaviour was born of insecurity, but that was hardly an excuse.

However, this was his employer, and it was none of his business. Michelle could leave when she'd had enough – just as he could once he couldn't stand this man any longer. He wouldn't even wait to be paid.

Silence.

Michelle didn't blush, nor did she show any sign of anger or frustration. It was a small triumph … or would it give Bernard licence to continue? Maybe he seldom spoke to her this way and it was merely a coincidence that Paul had heard two instances already. Whatever the case might be, he had to remember that she was, to an extent, equally responsible, because she kept herself in a position where it could continue happening. Certain comforts simply came with a price.

It really was none of his business.

'Where are we going?' he asked to cut the silence. The turn-off to Riebeek-Kasteel wasn't far away.

The deep voice from behind: 'Just go where I tell you.'

He had to nip that manner of speaking in the bud, and it would have to happen right now.

'Where you *ask* me to.'

The trick was to not sound irritated or give it a ring of admonishment, only make it a correction. He thought he had succeeded, but then he sensed the man's annoyance. When the reaction came, it was simply, 'Well then, I'm *asking* you to continue into town.'

Still, something approaching appreciation was evident. If you have a lot of money, you probably get used to everyone yessir-no-sirring you; then you start taking it for granted, but occasionally you probably get sick of it.

Paul took the exit. The church tower welcomed them.

The road curved into the town. Pretty place. Even over the engine's sophisticated purring you could hear a wholesome kind of silence. Here and there were some empty plots. Trees, shrubs, plants, flowers grew everywhere, and in the superlative.

'Left,' came a command-cum-request and Paul turned into Van Riebeeck Street. Way in the distance was a rise where the valley became a mountain.

'Right,' Bernard said. Now they were in Skool Street where, at the top of the hill, was a building that indeed could be nothing but a school. They didn't head in that direction, but turned left, into Piet Retief Street, before veering right. Up ahead they would have to turn left or right, Paul saw, otherwise they would end up in a vineyard.

A woman on the pavement put down her shopping bag. She seemed to be returning to the poorer part of town, but clearly needed a breather. She stared at the gleaming car and its occupants with open admiration.

They must be so happy, she was probably thinking.

13

The almost floor-length tablecloth was as immaculate as a virginal wedding dress. There wasn't a speck of dust to be seen anywhere in the restaurant, and Paul found it surprising that it was so empty – they were the only three takers for lunch. Despite the fact that the sun was shining brightly, Bernard had chosen to sit inside. Indeed, while Paul was lifting the wheelchair from the boot of the Mercedes, he had already started grumbling about not wanting the sunlight shining on his food.

After removing one of the chairs to allow Bernard to sit right up at the table, Michelle sat down to his right, not opposite him, therefore preventing Bernard from sitting in the middle. She probably wanted to make a point, but you couldn't quite put your finger on what that point was. It seemed to Paul the two were making up the rules as the battle went along.

It was a process of negotiation, at least. Bernard took something in exchange for every object he offered her on the material level, just as she gave him nothing for free.

Or that was Paul's deduction. Still, as these were two people who might yet turn out to have additional facets, he probably shouldn't try to sum up their relationship too soon.

There were two tables between them and the fireplace in which small flames flickered, but Paul could feel the heat right where he sat. With an 'It's cold here', Bernard had ensured that the window nearby had been shut.

Cesária Évora was singing in the background, so languidly that she sounded disinterested at times. Still lovely, though. But monotonous. One day, Paul thought, people would realise that Senhora Évora had only ever recorded around twelve songs, which she released in different orders, each time managing to convince the public it was a brand-new CD.

'It's a modest place really, Paul,' Bernard remarked after he had ordered wine on their behalf, 'but it has its surprises.'

Was that a meaningful glance he had given Michelle? If so, what might it mean? And what of that enigmatic smile of hers?

'The town, or this place?'

'Oh, this place.' Bernard waved his arm. 'Where you would be astonished by what you might find.' He laughed when he saw Paul looking at the menu; he hadn't been referring to the limited choice it offered. So to what, then?

Michelle put down her menu. 'Why don't you say it, Bernard? Then he'll be in the picture.'

Signs of irritation in her voice this time, and she had meant this to be noticeable. Lunch could turn into a long affair, Paul thought.

'I met Michelle here.' The look Bernard gave her was almost indifferent. 'She worked here.'

'As a waitress?' asked Paul.

A loud laugh. 'Well, she wasn't the manager!'

'I wasn't around long enough to become the manager.' Michelle's fingers caressed the salt-shaker, her short, dark nails so well manicured they must have been done professionally, and most likely not around here.

Bernard was distracted by the waiter arriving with the red wine. 'Ah, pour for us, pour for us ... no, I don't need to taste, it's the one I always have.' There was impatience in the way he held his glass for the waiter – probably not even twenty years old, the pale, gangly character sported a platoon of angry spots on his chin and a halting manner that betrayed his short tenure.

'Yes, sir.'

'Fill up.'

Bernard brought the glass to his lips without waiting for the rest of the table, took a mouthful, narrowed his eyes as he concentrated on the taste ...

It was the first of many such sips and three glasses later he was only just managing not to slur his words.

Up until now Bernard had done most of the talking, even when his mouth was full. Paul struggled to remember what had been said, because the man had the habit of jumping to a new topic before the current one had been exhausted or concluded. He had an opinion about everything under the sun, which was no surprise. Somewhere between it all there had been sideways references to how well things were going on the farm, how sought-after their grapes were, the success of his wine at a recent show. How difficult it was to find reliable labour, how the EFF was creating unrest by inciting local workers. Then on to how a certain eatery had gone downhill in Malmesbury, how weak the rand was, how ...

Out of the corner of his eye, Paul saw Michelle take a sip from her glass. *She* appeared to be the one with money, the one used to it all. Every now and then Bernard Russell was on the brink of being common.

And still Paul could *feel* her. He thought he was behaving normally, but his right side was aglow, the side closest to her. The real fire was right there beside him.

The waiter came to clear their plates. It was as if he hadn't noticed

Paul. 'I hope, sir, you and Mrs Russell had a good meal. Would you like to hear the dessert specials?'

Bernard's head turned. 'We are not ...'

The rest was unclear – his tongue didn't want to play along.

'Sorry, sir?'

'We're not married.'

Dear God, thought Paul.

'Sorry,' the lips mumbled from above the pimples.

'And I never have dessert. I didn't the last time when I was here, and that time you served us too.'

Ah, not a newbie, thought Paul, just a slow learner.

'I'm sorry.'

'Yes, yes.' Bernard waved him away like an insect. His cheeks had taken on a dark-pink tint, which looked odd paired with his dark eyes and eyebrows. 'Very many people have wondered if there will be another Mrs Russell. As if I would be stupid enough to tie the knot again!' He looked at Paul while speaking, but his sideways glance at Michelle made it clear where the barb was meant to strike.

Paul couldn't believe his ears – or, no, had it been a different couple, he realised, then he wouldn't have. He wanted to change the subject but found that nothing came to mind.

Yet it seemed a reaction was expected.

'Why *stupid*?' he asked.

First another sip of wine. 'Why take something you already have while giving up something else?'

'What would you be giving up, Bernard?' Michelle asked. For the first time Paul saw something welling in her. Her voice was even. She wasn't frowning. Her posture was relaxed. But it was there nevertheless. 'Money?' she asked lightly. 'Must be money. Everything is about money, after all.'

'Must be money.' He had a hard time forming his reply, and the words that followed. 'Paul, don't be in such a hurry.'

And here he was thinking his glimpse at his watch had gone unnoticed.

'Paul?' said Michelle.

'Hmm?'

'It was right here that I met Bernard. This very table.'

'Oh, really?'

'Well ...' That came from Bernard, who suddenly looked, well, cautious. This was the start of a new round, Paul sensed. Michelle wanted to turn the tables, even though her statement had sounded so innocent.

But nothing here was innocent.

'Bernard and his wife,' she informed him evenly. 'She was with him.'

He wanted to be elsewhere. This time yesterday there was still quiet in his life. Not happiness, not rest, not peace, but people weren't sniping at each other and trying to drag him into it. He was thinking that his first day on the job would have to be his last.

And then.

At first he thought he was imagining things.

But no, it was exactly what he had thought.

Her fingers on his knee, a light touch. Then more firmly – she squeezed the top of his knee.

Show nothing, he told himself. He just about had control over his face, but his body had its own agenda: heat coursed right through him. He could only hope Bernard was too pickled to realise what was going on, or too uncomfortable about the story Michelle was telling.

'And there I was, thinking "Who *is* this imposing man?"' She chattered away, giving no indication of what she was doing with her left hand, which had come to rest on Paul's thigh. 'And the beautiful woman with him? Then they told me it was Bernard Russell, and as I was taking care of their table, I had to be sure to provide them with the best service.'

'Michelle, I'm sure our driver isn't after that level of detail, and ...'

Had the bully really sounded so anxious? Paul's attention was elsewhere, however. It was on his right hand, which he oh-so casually moved to his lap, although it wanted to pounce straight onto hers – it was exerting the force of a huge magnet. Then he allowed it to slide under the tablecloth to graze hers.

'They were better dressed than the rest.' She turned her hand to grasp his, palm to palm. 'Or what was the word? Clothed. Noticeably better clothed.' She lifted Paul's hand and moved it up her leg. The thigh, right above the knee. He realised he was touching skin; she must have shifted up her dress. 'Bernard wasn't in the wheelchair yet, and his wife was very beautiful. Younger than him, I could tell. Much younger.' Her skin was warm, or was it the heat radiating from him? His cock was so hard he thought it might lift the table. 'Do you know, it's pretty odd. They expressly told me "that's Bernard Russell", but no one mentioned his wife's name. Later I discovered no one knew.' She moved his hand slightly higher. He thought he was going to explode. 'She was just "Mrs Russell", on a day out from the beautiful farm. She never came to town on her own.'

Bernard said nothing.

Paul thought that perhaps *he* should speak, but knew it was a bit much to ask when your brain wasn't the organ doing the thinking.

Still, he had to say *something*. He cleared his throat. Needed to try to get the conversation to more neutral ground anyway.

'If you're on a farm like Journey's End then you wouldn't have to get away too often.'

There. That wasn't too bad. Could stroke Bernard's ego, too.

He hoped that the tablecloth was long enough to hide what was going on. But the possibility that it *wasn't* and that someone might walk past and see what was going on ... well, that got him even harder.

'They said,' Michelle continued, 'Bernard Russell bought a farm here just to play.' Paul's arm was bent at an angle that was threatening to become excruciating, but his hand still wanted to move higher. 'And that he had more important things to do in Cape Town.' The tip of his middle finger touched the point where the elastic of her panties was taut. 'Things that the bunch of us here wouldn't be able to understand.'

When Bernard spoke, Paul's hand stopped moving. 'My affairs concern no one other than myself.'

The man leaned forward.

Paul removed his hand. Few things had ever been as difficult for him to do.

'People can be so inquisitive,' said Michelle. 'And they decide for themselves that a person's affairs might not be as straightforward as they should ...'

Paul's hand was back on the table, where it rested casually. He'd half-expected not to recognise it.

'Waiter,' Bernard called, and then louder, 'Waiter!' And before the bloke could get there, 'Another bottle. And see if this time you can be a little quicker?'

He had regained control of his speech. Started talking about how much better the region's peaches had been the previous year and that he was glad it wasn't his problem.

Paul nodded and appeared to be paying scant attention to the woman beside him.

But he wasn't in the least bit concerned about peaches.

The feeling he had supposed was gone forever was back, and unquestionably so: the desire to know what comes next. He couldn't read her mind. Was it just her way of paying Bernard back, humiliating him in front of another man without him knowing? Would any man have served the purpose?

She had read him like yesterday's paper, had known she could do it and there would be no repercussions, had known that he wouldn't remove her hand from his leg in annoyance.

The ugly premonition was still lurking, but he was too worked up to give it much consideration. It was just a couple of false notes emanating from his brain as it tried to start working again, and he didn't want it to spoil the symphony in his body.

Besides, he couldn't be *sure* everything would end badly.

14

'Are you afraid someone might be watching, Paul?' Lindsey asked. 'We're allowed to chat!'

He had looked back: even though they were among the vines, the house was still so big that it didn't feel far away. He knew where his bedroom window was, top left, but the tree concealed it.

Lindsey wanted to show him some of the farm, and the weather was ideal for a walk. The scent of the vineyard was so strong it felt as if he was at a wine tasting.

'Actually, I was wondering whether your father might be needing me again today.'

She shrugged her shoulders and her bitty breasts bobbed along under the mint-green dress. Her eyeshadow was the same colour.

'He would have said so. And he always takes an afternoon nap. Just not sure how much rest he gets with *her* there.'

Finally she had given enough of an indication that he could ask. 'You're not crazy about Michelle?'

'I ...' Lindsey came to a near-stop, stroked a perfect vine leaf, walked on. 'I have nothing against her.'

'Hmm.' He knew by now that when she went quiet, she wouldn't leave things at that.

'I might have felt this way about any ...'

'About any?'

'Oh. Whatever.'

'About any potential young stepmother?' he encouraged.

'There isn't any talk of me getting a stepmother yet!'

Her defence was too hasty. She was no longer looking up at him but gazing straight ahead, as if she was worried about tripping, even though the ground was more even here than the last stretch had been. Unlike Michelle, she was so easy to gauge.

Viewed objectively, she was equally attractive, albeit with a completely different aura and appearance, but still a stunner in her own right. Many young farmers in the district – and some of the older ones – must have wondered what it would be like to bag her. Despite her unaffectedness – or innocence, if such a thing still existed – the allure was there. Yes, objectively viewed, this girl might have been even more beautiful than the one he wanted, because a) there was gentleness to the package and b) most men aren't after trouble on two legs.

But he was neither objective nor someone who had ever known what was good for him.

Over and over, the sensation returned: Michelle's hand on his leg, his on hers. The way his body had responded and continued to do in her absence. It was like a chemical process in which an element that was neutral in isolation changed irrevocably on contact with another.

Lindsey might be first prize for many a man, but to him it was as good as telling someone with a sweet tooth that soup tasted better than chocolate.

'My father ...' she said suddenly.

'Hmm?'

'You know what men are like. He ...'

'No, I don't know. How?'

'You know!' She laughed. But she was immediately serious again. 'If she knew what she were doing, a woman could play with his mind. And my father isn't as hard a person as you might think.'

He didn't nod, but didn't contradict her either.

'He needs to make a lot of decisions.' Almost an excusing tone.

'You really don't know precisely what his job entails?'

'Just as I said.'

'Middleman.'

He didn't want to think her that naïve; Bernard Russell's business would certainly include illegal dealings. But people were the way they were raised to be. He could imagine how, over the years, Lindsey would have learnt that she could talk as much as she liked, but that there should be no unnecessary questions. She might just have unlearnt the desire to want to know more than she was told.

'Middleman and so on. Maybe Michelle knows more than I do. *She* would ask.' Again Lindsey looked at Paul, and he got the feeling she was going to make a further comment, but instead she said, 'You know, he wasn't always paralysed.'

He heard Michelle's voice again, in the restaurant:

Bernard wasn't in the wheelchair yet, and his wife was very beautiful.

He replied, 'I didn't know. How did it happen?'

'It was just me and him here, that day.' Lindsey's gaze was far away. 'Mary and Johnny were out buying things for the house. It was about three months ago. He ...'

He comes towards the top of the stairs, as usual. Will go down, as usual.

Today is different.

A foot catching on something, his right foot.

He doesn't know what he has caught it on, but he has lost his balance and is starting to fall.

Surprise on his face.

Shock.

He wants to grab the railing, but his fingers grasp at air.

The moment freezes, as does the sound he was about to make … and he himself seems frozen, hanging there. He almost wants to believe there is enough time to regain his balance, but then reality catches up with him, savagely.

'We don't quite know how it happened. He'd gone up and down those stairs so many times. But, well … I found him there, at the bottom. I could see he was never going to be the same again, I could just see it by the way … he was lying in a heap. At first I thought he was dead …'

Lindsey's throat sounded as if it was closing up and her eyes were red from keeping in the tears. Paul wanted to take her hand. Her delicate frame was made to be hugged, to be protected. But he knew that would be a mistake.

'And …?'

'Enough of this.' She shook her head. 'We can't change anything. It's just, sometimes I think … my father, fit as a fiddle. For something like that to happen to him, you know?'

'Hmm.'

They set off back home. Paul looked for a stirring at any of the curtains.

Nothing.

'I must admit my father needed someone like Michelle after that,' said Lindsey. 'Or maybe any woman.'

Suddenly there was a sound and they both looked over to where a dark-coloured BMW was coming towards them, moving faster than was prudent on a dirt road. In its wake, dust swirled in waves and even from where they were standing they heard the loud scrunching of gravel when the car came to a halt in front of the house.

A tall, slim man in his thirties – coloured or Portuguese – got out, his suit a dark pinstripe with a modern cut, his longish curly hair tied back in a ponytail. Boom! he slammed the car door. The way he hopped up the steps added to the conclusion Paul had already come to: dubious character.

From the dubious character's left hand dangled a light-grey briefcase that appeared to be made from the hide of some poor creature or other. He rang the doorbell.

'I thought your father was taking a rest,' Paul remarked. 'Someone you know?'

Lindsey frowned, a frown that said a lot. 'Just from seeing him around. It's one of his … acquaintances. Rodrigo or something. Don't know if that's his name or surname.'

Undoubtedly someone for whom Bernard was acting as go-between.

They saw Mary open the front door. It seemed no greetings were exchanged and that the man simply slid past her.

Lindsey sighed. 'Let me go see if they need anything. You enjoy the sun out here while you still can!'

Paul watched her go, the way her narrow hips swayed slightly as she walked. It would have been a great trespass to want the boss-man's daughter, oh yes. But not as bad as desiring his lover.

Then his eye caught a movement at the side of the house: Johnny, retreating round the corner.

He must have been standing there having a cigarette, Paul decided. The simple fact that he hadn't noticed the bloke earlier didn't mean that Johnny had been watching them. And even if he had, there'd been nothing fishy to see.

Lindsey disappeared through the front door.

And him? He didn't feel like going in yet, even though he was curious about the kind of business under discussion. It would probably be taking place in Bernard's study, in any case. It was much more refreshing outdoors than inside that house with all its undercurrents.

He took a seat on the veranda, a short way from the front door, with his back to the wall. Sat looking into the distance, and looking inside himself.

15

He hadn't been on the veranda for long before he decided to go inside after all. It was only half past four, but the valley had started to cool down and he suspected the temperature would plummet that night.

He reckoned he would be spending most of his days in uniform, hanging around to see whether Bernard wished to be ferried somewhere. He would receive his three meals and have a little chat here and there. But with whom? He had to avoid leading Lindsey on, alone time with Michelle was an idea as good as launching a nuclear weapon, and neither Mary nor Johnny was what he would call a first-rate conversationalist.

He closed the front door and turned towards the empty hallway. Was *she* around?

It was irrelevant. He was going to stop brooding over what had happened in the restaurant – enough time had passed for him to be able to think about it logically. It was a slip-up; they were both at fault. Bernard was his employer. Michelle's too, so to speak. She had much more to lose than he did. Yes, it was useless denying she had a certain effect on him, why exactly he couldn't say, but nothing could come of it. He had to be sure to keep a similar situation from arising. If it seemed it might happen, he would have to prove to himself that he had some degree of self-control.

Moreover, he was increasingly sure she had merely used him in much the way that an unarmed soldier on the point of defeat suddenly sees and seizes a sharp object of which the overconfident enemy is unaware. That Bernard was clueless as to what had been happening must have made the victory so much sweeter. But he, Paul, was not one of the combatants; it was their war. Michelle had already accomplished her goal, while he would have been in the running for Idiot of the Year had he viewed it as an indication of things to come.

He felt better now that he had worked it all out.

The house was quiet, maybe partly because there was business taking place. Should he go to his room and stay there until it was time for supper?

Deciding not to, he stepped into the lounge instead.

Where he stopped in his tracks, because Michelle was standing in front of the liquor cabinet. She didn't turn around, but the positioning of her shoulders showed him she was aware of his presence. Otherwise he would have retreated.

'Did the two of you have a nice walk?'

Her husky voice was breathy now too; clearly she didn't want anyone to hear them. Dead-ordinary question, but he wondered whether she had been watching them. Could she be jealous? Despite all his reasoning a moment ago, this was an exciting thought.

If she was, then good! But here he was, in her presence for just a few seconds and already his resolution wasn't quite so firm. His hand itched to be able to settle on the same place it had been earlier today.

'Lindsey wanted to show me ...'

She gestured twice: a wave to cancel further explanation and another towards the brandy and glasses.

'Are you going to have a little something to drink with me? The important people are upstairs discussing important matters.'

'All of them?'

'Bernard and his guest. Lindsey is somewhere up there too. Those are the important people.' Her hand was resting on the bottle, waiting.

'No thanks. But help yourself.'

'Oh, I *will*. How can one be in the Boland and not drink anything?'

This was their first time alone. The feeling was getting stronger, all the things storybooks promised, the clichés that remained as valid as when they had been first created: the coming together of Yin and Yang, the two halves that complete each other, opposites attracting.

All this he had to ignore.

'Listen, Michelle, in the restaurant ...'

She took a swig. 'It mustn't happen again?'

'Exactly.'

Her look told him she knew better. She stroked her neck absent-mindedly, and immediately he wanted to place his hand there.

'I hear you.' Another sip. She looked at the liquid in her glass, looked at him. 'Did you leave the police because of a drinking problem?'

'How would you know I was in the police? Did Lindsey tell you?'

'I didn't need anyone to tell me. I knew it soon enough.'

Paul grinned. 'What do you mean? You had a lot of cops put their hands up your dress?'

She came closer. Closer still, a metre from him.

'Who knows? Yes, maybe I've had more than one cop copping a feel.'

She placed her hand lightly not on the lapel of his jacket, but on the white shirt. On his chest. She looked directly at him. She let her thumb tease his nipple.

He inhaled sharply. Even if he kept telling her until his voice caved that nothing could happen again, they both knew all it took was one touch like that for any such resolve to fly out the window.

Then Michelle stepped away quickly. She looked over his shoulder and Paul turned slightly. Saw Mary moving past the open door.

He was probably meant to feel guilty, and he did, for a second, but then he shrugged. As he started to leave, Michelle's voice trailed after him, still breathy:

'There are eyes and ears wherever you turn, aren't there? Right, I'll let you go. For now.'

16

Mary knew that sort of look. The kind that needed to be cut short as soon as possible.

Now, while she supervised Johnny trimming the fat to her instructions and then coating the mutton chops in flour, it was that look that stayed with her. She had nothing against the man. Paul whatsisname. Mullan, Paul Mullan. She didn't have an issue with where he came from or where he was going; he could be on his way to Mars for all she cared. But that shine of his eyes ... she wanted to convince herself she'd only imagined it. But she *had* seen it, and no wonder. What kind of man wouldn't have a girl like that catch his eye?

She'd got that feeling yesterday, when he arrived here – didn't know him from Adam, but recognised the kind of trouble his sort always had in store. You felt it rather than being able to verbalise it, and you couldn't be specific about the kind of trouble either until it was upon you. Today it was still nothing more than interest, but it would take root with a vengeance unless it was weeded out immediately. But she couldn't do that. She couldn't say anything without proof.

If enough of those looks were exchanged, nothing would be the same again. Nobody knew that better than she.

She couldn't think about that now. *Would* not!

But the memories came flooding back. The ones that threatened to haunt her anew every evening unless she downed the glass on the nightstand, squeezed her eyes shut and got everything other than the sound of her breathing out of her head.

Memories of the time she should have opened her mouth.

The daughter of Johannes and Grieta Fortuin, product of the Cape Flats. Fortuin! What a joke, because no one would have thought of describing the combined income of the parents of that little coloured girl as a fortune, and today she still had nothing. Just the fancy name – Mary – because shortly before she was born her mother had read something about Queen Mary. She was an only child; there was trouble with the delivery and her mother would never bear children again. 'I could have had a son,' Grieta often sighed. Mary was no boy, nor was she the dainty little thing a daughter was supposed to be. A son might have been able to get an after-school education and get out of the Flats and send money home. And more than that – take them away to a better place.

Her father never stepped in when Grieta scolded her about sweet bloody nothing, even though he loved her. She could see it in his eyes. Like Mister Bernard, who didn't show his feelings either. Most men had that problem. Johannes Fortuin was also a big strong man like Mister Bernard, or the way Mister Bernard was before. You would think Johannes Fortuin could thump everything and everyone out of his way. You'd never believe his wife wore the pants the way she did.

He was too in love with Grieta, *that's* what. Too blind.

The years passed. Mary became older. A teenager.

She was blind herself. It was nothing, really, when Johannes's brother moved in. It would only be a week, maybe two; there had been a misunderstanding at the place he was meant to go. Uncle

Peter. His name was Pieter in reality, but somewhere in all the moving around he became Peter. Would only speak English, even though his accent was as strong as Mary's own.

Grieta suddenly switched over to English too. Mary even heard her introduce herself to someone as 'Ghreta' once until the woman next door laughed out loud, and then she never tried it again.

There were long conversations between Uncle Peter and Grieta, just the two of them, about what he had seen in the rest of the country. It bothered Mary that she and her father were excluded, as they also sat in the little lounge every evening. She thought she had no right to feel this way; if anyone ought to be upset, it should be her father, but he wasn't, because she would have noticed. Even though he never showed any emotions, she still would have seen.

One day, about a year later, she got a heavy nosebleed at school. She was in Grade Ten, it was the last term, and she didn't really want to go home. She was worried she would miss too much, what with final exams being so soon, but the front of her blouse was covered in red, red blood, and Miss Pringle told her to go. 'I know you're not faking it, you're not like the others who would do anything to miss a day's school, it's fine, see you tomorrow,' she'd said.

When she got home Mary saw Uncle Peter's little van parked out front. But at breakfast that morning he'd said he had some big things to do in Muizenberg. A tall tale, then. She didn't want him to hear she was back, because then he would tell Grieta when she got in from her job manning the till at the café, so she crept around the side of the house. The window of her small room was closed, but she could open it from outside if she pushed the right place in the right way.

She didn't get that far. From her mother and father's bedroom window, which was slightly ajar, she heard Grieta laugh.

Uncle Peter, too.

It took Mary a few seconds to realise what that and the other sounds meant. Some of her classmates had so much to say about that kind of thing; she'd no real idea what it would sound like when you really did it, but now she knew it sounded like this.

She started running, but stopped suddenly several blocks later. Wiped away her tears. She had been stupid. She was such a child, a bloody child, she was a fucking blind child, having ignored so much. The signs had been there the whole time. How long had Uncle Peter been reaming her mother? Was it weeks? Months? Had it started soon after he moved in? She remembered she *had* seen the looks they exchanged.

She would have to tell her father. It would be terrible, but she would have to.

But she didn't do it that day. Or the following. And then the days went by, and she said nothing. Where would you start? Furtively she watched Uncle Peter and Grieta, but it was too late. She told herself her father probably knew, that he'd made peace with it, and that she'd make everything worse by mentioning it to him.

He knew, she decided, when she watched him. But he carried on. People could adjust to anything. And Grieta hadn't scolded either of them in a while, so in a way things were better. Her father must have been feeling he'd gained more from the situation than he'd lost. And it was his brother, wasn't it, so he had to forgive them. She didn't want to let it all run through her head. These were grown-up things and he was her father. And Grieta was her mother, even if Mary hated her. She wished everything could start from the beginning so that she could have done something about those glances.

The kind Paul Mullan was dishing out here.

And the one who was returning them.

He should only have been staying a night, but now it was longer. It didn't matter that she actually rather liked him; he had to leave, and soon. Had Uncle Peter spent just the one night with them in the Cape Flats, that might have been the end of the story.

And then she would never have woken up at four o'clock one morning with the immediate realisation that something was wrong. She *knew*, even though there wasn't a sound in the neighbourhood that became so rowdy at times. It was the kind of waking that happened when you heard something fall and break.

She went out into the passage. Everything was fine.

Then something told her: Go to the garage.

She opened the door and turned on the light – and saw her father asleep at the wheel. Mary wanted to laugh. He'd given her such a fright! She wanted to get in beside him and chat away like they hadn't in a long time.

Then she became aware of all that was wrong. The sharp smell in the air that was making her eyes burn. All the car windows wound up, apart from the one opened just enough to let the hosepipe through. The angle at which his head was hanging.

Then she knew it wasn't just once she should have spoken up and didn't, it was twice. She could have prevented this thing, everything could have been different if her father had known earlier, or if he had been able to share with someone what he had realised.

She just waited for the funeral to be over and then she ran away from home. Those two could have each other, the whores. A man could be a whore too. They whored her father to death and she'd be damned if she'd ever give a fuck for a man.

But knowing them, that was different. She *knew* them. Recognised that look on their faces when it arrived. Like Johnny had these last weeks, here in the house in which Mister Bernard trusted him. Johnny even looked at the *two* of them at once: Michelle *and* Lindsey, both Mister Bernard's. Everything here was Mister Bernard's, and that was as it should be. Didn't he take care of them all? She would never forget how he took her in when she came knocking at the old house in Cape Town without any references. He has been through enough in the last while. He gave her a job and a place to stay when she had nowhere to go, and now it was her turn to look out for him. He wasn't always as observant as he thought.

She'd had a little word with Mister Bernard in private and at first there was nothing, but then yesterday evening he put Johnny in his place.

She watched Johnny starting to fry the chops.

'Don't do them to death,' she ordered. 'Just golden brown. Then you add that stuff.'

Johnny didn't look where she was pointing, just grunted.

'Johnny, did you hear?'

'I heard.'

He had to know where he stood, and oh, did he know it now! Nobody could put another person in their place the way Mister Bernard could, once he knew what was what.

And now this Paul, with the kind of thoughts that set people on the wrong path. Bloody hell! Did you have to have eyes everywhere?

17

The melody was soothing, but the volume quite high. It was Albinoni's breathtaking 'Adagio', one of the few Baroque pieces Paul knew by name – most of the compositions from that era he found rather similar, too ornamental to his taste.

Compromises had to be made if you wanted the best, because the shiny, ultramodern hi-fi clashed with all the subdued antiques, and while the speakers were well designed, their angular shape was irreconcilable with the deep-red couch and the elegant lines of the chairs.

Supper had come and gone, but Bernard suggested everyone sit down and enjoy a glass of something in the lounge.

Over there was where Michelle had been standing that afternoon, Paul thought looking at the liquor cabinet. He remembered the feel of her fingers on his chest, stroking the cotton of his shirt.

Now she was seated close to Bernard, who was in his wheelchair. She was laughing about something he'd said, but he had no idea what, as the man was speaking softly for a change. Paul was sitting so close to one of the speakers that everything else was drowned out by the sound of the organ, violins and other string instruments.

And then there was the crackling fire.

This was good, because he wasn't in the mood for talking. The others left him alone; it was just him and a big glass of red wine, initially three-quarters full but emptying steadily.

Bernard puffed on a cigar, making grey clouds over his head, and the aroma filled the room. Looking at them you would think there had never been a moment's tension between the two. Paul knew she was an accomplished actress, but Bernard surprised him; if he still had any ill feeling towards her, there was no trace of it. And now he was laughing at something *she* had said.

Paul doused the jealousy inside himself … or he tried to. This was probably the way things normally were between them, with only occasional conflict; Michelle wouldn't find herself ensconced in luxury for long if she didn't keep her lover happy most of the time. And he, Paul, what was *he*? Was the tease all this was about, or was she one of those women who just needed to be desired?

Lindsey and Johnny were chatting, and he didn't get the gist of that either. Johnny had entered the room about two minutes earlier, bathed in the aroma of Chesterfield; it seemed Bernard was the only one allowed to smoke inside. Lindsey was doing most of the talking.

'They are beautifully soft but unnecessarily expensive,' Paul heard her say as the music stopped. Johnny nodded, though it was probably about women's clothes.

The next track started. This one he also knew: 'Air on the G String'.

Bernard said something. Michelle smiled and rested her hand on his arm.

Lindsey looked at them and bit the inside of her left cheek, saw Paul had noticed and smiled at him.

He let his gaze wander; looked back over at Michelle.

Who wasn't looking at him. He couldn't remember when last she *had*, tonight.

He noticed that Johnny was watching him. He frowned and Johnny looked away.

Mary had moved in like a corpulent phantom to summon Johnny. His help was clearly needed. Half-irritated, half-embarrassed, he got up. Paul saw Lindsey look at him in sympathy. Mary sailed back to the kitchen – working the swing door with her shoulder – and Johnny followed in her wake.

Lindsey got up. 'I'm going to get some air.'

Bernard and Michelle both nodded, still deep in conversation.

He didn't want to sit there watching them for one more second. He kept his eyes looking downwards, listening to the music, which was starting to get on his nerves. Now he'd rather they were fighting again. He couldn't stand seeing her this way with the older man; it made it too obvious what the rest of the evening had in store.

He was damn jealous and it was getting worse. *He* had to be the one with her. In any case, with the man not having use of his legs, how did they manage to fuck?

There was a time he wouldn't have been able to sit like this, not in the days when he needed to assert himself wherever he went. Lizzy-who-fell-pregnant wasn't the only casualty; girls were a particular source of contention.

How he once would have got stuck in for the one sitting close by now!

Anyone who didn't believe in winning or losing had, in his opinion, been a loser. It was no shame to fight and *then* lose – as long as it was temporary. He was neither the strongest nor the tallest in his class, even less so in his school, but even so he was up for guys who had already left. Of course he'd lost sometimes, but he'd waited for another opportunity – no one could stay on their guard forever – and then he would put things right with a stick or a stone or a piece of metal piping. It was difficult to boast about how you'd taught Paul Mullan a lesson if you no longer had all your front teeth.

In Steven Doyle's case it was a canine that was lost. His had been prominent, almost exactly like the kind you saw in vampire movies, where they extended before the victim got bitten. And the fight was over a girl, one whose name Paul couldn't remember. Or that was the official reason, because the fight between him and Steven, who was two years older, had been brewing for a long time. She was going steady with Steven when Paul asked her out. He knew she'd say no because she had a boyfriend. So he didn't blame her for that, but called her a cock-teasing whore all the same because he knew she would go complaining to Steven.

Which is precisely what happened. The next day Steven Doyle started shoving him around behind the school sheds, two of his cronies in tow. But next minute Steven was the one to get shoved around, seen to, fucked up. And there went a Dracula tooth, bouncing off the shed with a ping! Steven was left sitting in the dirt with his hand clamped to his bloody mouth. One of the spectators was smoking and holding a matchbox – Paul took it from him, shook out the matches, put the tooth inside, stuffed the box in his pocket and walked away. His knuckles stung where they had been cut, but while they healed soon enough, Steven couldn't get his tooth back. Each time Paul walked past him in the corridor, he took the box out of his pocket and shook it for the guy to hear.

Rattle-rattle.

What an arsehole he had been. Like a moth, only not attracted by light, but by darkness. If he could have stuck to a schedule, you would have been able to sell tickets to his fights.

But Bernard Russell was not Steven Doyle. And even if the Paul Mullan of today was still the one of days gone by, he wouldn't have fought a guy in a wheelchair.

If only there was an easy 'solution'. Even when he had been a policeman, with threat ever near, he missed that release. The way you could get rid of anger and frustration in a scuffle that would be over in minutes. It was so addictive being in that socially unacceptable but occasionally justifiable zone. No wonder he could outwit criminals. He had as much of a criminal past as the most of them!

He tried not to look, but nevertheless remained intensely aware of Bernard's hand on Michelle's arm. The light grasp of an owner.

It should have been *him* over there with her.

But when last had he been with a woman? It had been Sandra in Pretoria, long before What Happened, before his sex drive took off along with any and every other kind of pleasure in the aftermath of that terrible night. Not once in any of the towns or cities where he had spent the night since had he felt the urge to seek any such release.

Now all this newfound energy wanted out.

Paul got up. 'Night, both.'

Polite nods before they continued talking.

Out in the hallway he didn't get so far as turning towards the staircase.

'Paul.'

The front door was half-open and from the veranda Lindsey gestured for him to come closer.

'Won't you catch cold?' he asked.

'Come see the stars.'

It might be calming, he figured, so he went outside and closed the door behind him. The sounds of Baroque music were cut off abruptly, now there was just silence.

And the stars above.

It was something to behold, with so many more stars than in the city. Clearer, closer. You could be hypnotised if you kept staring.

Neither of them spoke. And it did calm him. Evenings alone with Lindsey would make a man feel good. No storms. She was soft, she was approachable, she would always be obliging. She even knew how much perfume to wear, because he was aware of the fragrance without it being prominent.

'Times like this I don't miss the city,' she noted softly.

'But other times you do?'

She kept looking up. 'You know … nothing else can make you feel this small. Reminding you how little one can actually plan. I mean, things happen, whether you plan or not. What is that saying? "Man makes plans, and God laughs." Or something like that.'

Paul thought about how Bernard and Michelle would soon be heading upstairs, to their bedroom. He had chosen to stay here mainly to be near her, and God found this amusing?

'People have a say too,' he told Lindsey. He had to quibble. He would not accept that everything simply happened the way it was supposed to. 'You don't just allow everything.'

'Sometimes I wonder,' she said, with a hint of sadness in her voice. It looked as if she wanted to turn away, then she looked back at him, almost sharply, almost confrontationally, but he could tell she was really dealing with something inside. 'Has anyone told you about my mother?'

'No?'

'She …' Lindsey looked towards the front door, but it was still closed. 'There aren't things like secrets around here anyway. My mother …'

She walks out the bedroom, the woman. A beautiful woman, more than twenty years Bernard Russell's junior.

A woman prone to dark moods, some days more than others. Today in particular.

In fact, it has never been this bad.

In the passage she listens to hear whether there is anyone around. No. She walks to the study and opens the door. Empty, as she knew it would be.

She closes the door, goes to the desk and opens a drawer. There it is, the pistol.

Her solution.

With shaking hands she takes it from the drawer, sits down in Bernard's chair, takes a deep breath and brings the cold barrel to her temple.

'That was about four months ago.' Lindsey's voice broke. 'Just a month before my father's accident, on the stairs, when he … So many things have happened since we moved here.'

Paul felt uncomfortable, but could hardly ask her to stop talking. He was learning too much about these people too quickly, he thought.

'She was never diagnosed with depression,' Lindsey continued. 'She didn't want to acknowledge that she had it. And my father always waved the idea aside. Until the afternoon she did it. My father always kept the pistol in the drawer. Still does. Everyone knew it was there.'

Even now? Paul wanted to ask, surprised, but he kept quiet.

The tears had started coming. 'We don't know what led to her doing it. Who could have guessed? But we should have been able to foresee it, because when someone suffers from depression, you can't have a gun in the house. But we *did*, and so …'

Paul took the crying girl in his arms. It was a natural reaction. Equally natural was the way her head rested on his shoulder.

She gulped. 'You must be thinking, especially you, being so good at keeping things to yourself: Who's this girl who spills her guts just like that? My past, everyone's … It's no use to me to keep thinking about it, anyway.'

'Nobody chooses what they remember.'

He'd barely said the words when he wished *he* could forget.

Then his eye caught a movement behind them to the right. Mary at one of the lounge windows, her hand on the curtain. She might have been standing there a while. The light was behind her, her face in shadow.

Suddenly self-conscious, Paul stood aside as Lindsey wiped her eyes.

The curtain closed.

18

His room was the place to which he escaped, or that was his intention, but when he closed the door and locked it, she was there. He stood still, his hand on the key. Her presence behind him.

He turned around, truly believing that the movement would bring her into the circle of his embrace.

'Michelle,' he wanted to say.

Nothing. No bedroom had ever looked emptier.

But she was everywhere. Since he had come back indoors, he anticipated her presence around every corner, and so he *felt* her around every corner. She was the injured toe you kept stubbing, the tune you couldn't get out of your head.

He didn't want to either. Then again, yes. And then not.

It was a feeling as imperative as an itch in need of immediate scratching; even worse, because it came from within. It wasn't just his brain sending out signals, his entire body was on red alert, organs pumping as they hadn't done in ages, hairs on the back of his neck permanently standing on end, ears pricked, eyes searching, fingers stroking his own skin the way he wanted them to glide over hers ...

Fuck it, you're not a schoolboy! But he remained one great itch, from his head that should have known better to his nagging dick, down to the feet he could have used to get lost, as he knew he should.

He flopped down on his bed. It wasn't quite ten, he couldn't try to go to sleep yet – unless she would be waiting in another dream the way she haunted his thoughts as he moved through the house. Maybe she could replace those *other* images.

He wasn't even blinded by who and what she was. He was realistic, he knew very well she wasn't perfect. A companion to a rich old man. By this time she would surely have as few illusions as he did, and any guy knows to go for the girl who still has a few intact, especially when it comes to men. But he wanted to save her before she lost even more, before she became just like him.

These were ridiculous arguments, he knew, but at long last he was thinking about such things again; in fact, he couldn't stop thinking. Ever since this afternoon he had been imagining all sorts of conversations – and situations – with her. If he turned over now, he would bump into her, and he would put out his hand to stop her from falling off the bed, and it wouldn't be her arm but her breast he touched, and he would start apologising before he saw the way she was looking at him. And, and, and.

She was in no need of saving, he realised, but the instinct to want to was part of it, a small noble idea that meant that not all of this was a lascivious cliché.

There was something else: Michelle could be *his* salvation. He had a goal again. He had been falling and falling the entire time and now, all at once, it felt as if there was hope of him landing somewhere.

He looked at his watch. Seven seconds to ten. He would try to sleep.

19

Somewhere in the dark early-morning hours – as dark as it could get in a place where the stars seemed so close – he did manage to sleep, but restlessly and not for long.

Images.

Again, the same images.

But they always stopped when he woke up, like now. There was enough moonlight coming through the window, even past the oak, for him to see his midriff was glistening with sweat. He had long given up wearing anything to bed so that only the sheets got punished. Some mornings, on leaving a guest house or hotel where the nightmares only arrived shortly before it was time to wake up, he wondered what the cleaner would make of the clammy bedlinen.

He was still catching breath. It had been so realistic.

It always was.

The worst was when he woke up and thought it was just a dream – and for a few seconds he could believe that – and then it hit home: you can wish as much as you like, but if something has changed you that much it will always forever be a part of your life. The repetition, the predictability, made it no less upsetting.

Once in a while he woke up without the images in his mind, as when any other person awoke after a dream-free night. Then he was grateful. You had to find your little joys and appreciate them. He was also happy each time the sun rose and he had another day to wedge between the nights.

He heard a sound and realised this was what had woken him.

The doorknob turned and the door swung open slowly.

She appeared. It was too dark to see her face, but from the length and fall of her hair and the neckline of the white nightdress he knew it was her. She came closer. Now he could make out more, including how she held her finger up in front of her mouth.

The moment wasn't right, but nothing could make any difference to how he felt when she pulled the nightdress over her head, let it fall and sunk down next to him.

He grabbed her. It nearly turned into a wrestling match in the way they immediately tried to get enough of each other, flesh on flesh, and it felt exactly the way he had thought it would. He could hear his own harsh breathing; hers as well.

Then, a fright, one that left him unable to breathe.

There was something cold against his temple, something she was holding. And then he realised *what*: a barrel pressed up against his temple, probably just about where Lindsey's mother …

He blinked. No, his eyes flew open. He was alone in a sweaty bed. He swung round to look at the door.

He was panting, but started to get his breath under control. He got up and went to the door to check that it really was locked.

Of course it was. Jesus Christ. As if the nightmare hadn't been enough, this place was stirring up even more in him.

He lay down and decided he would at least rest if he really couldn't sleep. Closed his eyes. Rubbed his stomach.

Imagined it was her hand. It started moving down.

Rock hard.

He opened his eyes and looked at the empty half of the bed. She's lying asleep next to another man, pal.

He closed his eyes again, and then he was in the passage.

The woman emerges from the bedroom. A beautiful woman, but she looks older than she is. He sees her close up and can't believe that she is unaware of him next to her – otherwise she would have somehow shown it.

She hesitates in the passage, listens to check whether anyone might be able to hear her, and then walks over to the study.

Goes in.

Now he can only see her head and shoulders – that's how close he is. He opens his mouth … Keeps right behind her. What did he want to say? Oh yes. The order is wrong. She closes the door behind her as she was meant to, but goes to sit at the desk without having first opened the drawer.

Yet the barrel of a pistol is already at her temple.

He steps backwards to get a full view.

It is Michelle grasping the pistol. The nail of the finger that slowly curls more tightly around the trigger is so well manicured, it must be the work of a beautician.

Then, a voice. 'I must admit my father needed someone like Michelle after that. Or maybe any woman.'

The look on the face of the woman holding the pistol can only be described as evil.

A shot rings out.

There is an echo.

And another.

He whipped up in bed, awake, this time truly awake. All was quiet, apart from his panting that by rights should have wrenched everyone in the house out of their dreams, no matter how well sealed the doors were.

He pressed a button on his watch and saw the time was 03:41. Sigh. He rolled away from the sweat-soaked sheet under him to a cool, dry part of the bed. He wondered about the odd outline of something on the desk, before he realised it was the vase of white roses Mary had placed there. He also made out the angular form of his suitcase, open and in the same position as yesterday, full of clothes he still hadn't put in the wardrobe.

DAY 3

20

He was still tired when he sat down at the dining table, alone in the room. It was just after seven, but he was more than done with the bed, which resembled a modern-art project the way things had been twisted and tangled.

Again, he left it as it was.

Hopefully the sun would give him the same lift it did the surroundings. Through one of the windows, open just a few centimetres, came the delighted chirping of a bird.

The swing door opened. Mary shouldered her way into the dining room, feather duster in hand.

'Morning,' said Paul.

She looked him over as if she were inspecting the chauffeur's uniform rather than the person inside. Then he was offered a nod, after which she started dusting the silverware on the buffet. He wouldn't have thought it necessary, but she probably did it every day.

Swish, swish. She swung the thing like a conductor with a baton.

Again the swing door. This time it was Johnny. Paul only realised how hungry he was when the plate was deposited in front of him.

Ka-plunk. Even with the delightful aroma of bacon, eggs and toast, the smell of tobacco that hung on the man like a cloak was all-pervasive.

'Sorry you had to wait, man of mystery.'

He'd had it with the eternal sarcasm, and due to the lack of rest he'd be damned if he was going to keep his mouth shut.

'That's quite all right, Johnny, thank you. Everybody knows the help of today isn't what it once was.'

The bloke froze. Paul knew he was at risk in his seated position; if ever Johnny was going to give him a good old-fashioned backhander it would be now.

To settle the point that there were more pressing matters at hand than who had brought him his plate, he started dissecting a piece of bacon with great care.

Johnny set off for the kitchen, rod up his arse.

His food certainly tasted good though.

Mary still had her back to Paul, but her stance and the angle of her head showed she was amused. Not that she had interrupted her rhythmic dusting for a moment.

Footsteps came from the stairway. Paul was instantly more awake. High heels. Naturally it could be either of the women, but the way his body was responding had already told him which one it was.

Michelle went to sit in the chair opposite him. 'Morning, um, Paul ... Morning, Mary.'

Returning the greeting, he had to admit it was smart to pretend that she couldn't remember his name immediately. If his name honestly wasn't foremost in her mind, he'd be less pleased.

'Mary,' she asked pleasantly, 'look at me quickly? Then I'll be sure you will hear me.'

The older woman turned around slowly. She would never say out loud that Michelle only enjoyed a measure of authority for Bernard's sake. But it was in her every movement.

'I'm looking, Miss Michelle. What is it?'

'Mister Bernard has a migraine. But don't worry yourself over it. I've already given him something.'

'Yes, Miss.'

'He'll probably stay in bed all morning.'

And there it was. He wasn't imagining things. Michelle's eyes met his fleetingly, pretend-casual. She was sending a message, making a suggestion.

'All right,' Mary said. 'Mister Bernard needs his rest, then.'

Michelle's eyes met his again. 'Probably all morning.'

He was careful to show nothing other than polite concern, but inside he was a maelstrom. It was now or never. Stand down, his head cautioned. Let it go before you get your fingers burnt. But to get them burnt on someone like this!

Even if it *were* to end badly, well, you pays yer money and you takes yer chances, he thought. He would take a risk for a change. *Do* something.

Every moment seemed an eternity now that he knew they were headed somewhere. First he had to finish eating. Bite by bite. And then he was done, but Johnny had just arrived and now Michelle had a plate of food in front of her. They didn't speak.

Mary made her exit, but Johnny stood waiting next to the swing door. He didn't look towards the table but stared straight ahead. He must have chosen a spot on the wall to focus on.

Paul and Michelle, two people opposite each other, one eating and one with a cup of coffee. So many minutes still to come and go. It seemed to Paul that the hands of the cosmological clock were being held back by a gang of demons.

He placed his cup in the saucer and got up. He had to phrase it innocently.

'Seeing as it seems my services won't be necessary this morning, I'm going to take a walk.'

He noticed Johnny looking at him and then looking away again. Paul signalled quickly: he put his hand to his chest, five fingers spread.

Five minutes.

Michelle nodded lightly.

He flicked his eyelids to direct her: upstairs.Then he headed to the front door. Outside, sunlight and greenery. Everything was fresh. His heart was going wild. He didn't want to encounter anyone who could delay him. And there should be no witnesses to what he was doing; as far as he knew there were no labourers around and he could only hope no one was close enough to the house.

As he walked he kept his eyes peeled. Not a soul. Much as he wanted to, he managed to stop himself from looking back. Where was Lindsey? Still asleep? Mary was inside, but he didn't know if she was in the kitchen.

This is your last chance to change your mind, his brain nagged. Don't do it, you're asking for trouble. Go back inside!

Last chance? To hell with that. He knew he shouldn't, but he'd been trying to do the right thing for so long, and it hadn't helped. She belonged to another man, even if it was someone who was merely renting her, and it was shameless wanting to do something like that under this man's roof. And even though all is fair in love and war, there would be hell to pay if Bernard ever found out. But then they just had to make sure he never did.

Paul got to the oak tree and looked up at his bedroom window, open like he had left it. When had he last climbed a tree? Even as a child he'd not had much opportunity. He wasn't particularly afraid of heights; he just had to prevent himself ruining the uniform.

First he peered through a window on the ground floor. Everything was dark inside, too dark to distinguish much besides the outlines of two chairs. Perhaps it was a storeroom. All that mattered was that there was no one inside.

Paul started climbing. It was easy, or his effervescence made it seem that way. There were enough branches to grab. The bark was hard and rough under his fingers and chafed his palms.

Suddenly it wasn't so easy. The next branch that looked fit to carry his weight was far away.

Bugger it. He reached up, pulled himself onto a branch that curved upwards, praying that it wouldn't break, and then stretched even further, wishing his fingers were longer ...

Gotcha!

Then his foot slipped; either his sole was too worn or the branch was too smooth.

Instinctively, he tightened his grip.

His body jerked as he dangled in mid-air.

Still he hung on, his grasp solid enough.

He wouldn't be able to hold on much longer, though, so he grabbed at the branch with his left hand – he'd have to hang on with both hands.

But he missed it, his hand had swept too low. He swayed.

He had one more chance before he'd have to let go and tumble to the ground. It was now or never.

This time he got hold of the branch with both hands. Felt for that lower branch with his feet. There! He was sure both feet were balanced, and although he might well slip again, this time he was expecting it.

He was climbing again, faster. And then he was there. He grasped the windowsill, then the window itself. The tree was so close to the wall that it was simply a case of climbing over and then pulling himself through.

He slid into his room like a reptile, then slumped onto the floor.

He was in!

His heart was beating wildly, but there was no time to recover. How much time had passed? He couldn't leave Michelle waiting in the passage, or risk her leaving!

He got up, weaved his way to the bed and tugged at the tangle of sheets. Why hadn't he tidied them earlier? On his way over to the door he bumped into the desk and had to stop the vase from falling over. He took the key from his pocket and put it in the keyhole just as there was a light knock.

He turned the key and yanked the door open. She came inside and he closed it hastily, his hand shaking lightly. He locked it, but the key fell out, clap-a-clap onto the wooden floor. He wanted to pick it up at first, but fuck it, he decided.

Besides, she had taken him by the hand and was leading him to the bed.

They fell down onto it.

All those clothes had to go. They weren't just at their own but also each other's, and were in such a hurry to get rid of them that it was more of a hindrance than a help.

But finally all that was left was a slip of black lace through which he could feel how wet she was, and then it was just two naked bodies together. She was a perfect creature, this was too good to really be happening, but she wasn't acting like any goddess, more like the kind of girl his mother would have warned him against, had she not been too coy. This girl was a stranger to coyness and moaned in his ear as he pressed her tightly to him.

And then he let go, because he wanted to look at her again. He had to take it all in, take mental pictures. Her breasts, designed to be touched, filled his hands. She stroked her way down his stomach until she could feel how hard he had become for her.

It was happening. It was really happening. This time he wasn't going to wake up to find himself alone in the dark.

As he entered her she cried out so loudly that he was briefly concerned about the room keeping sound in as well as it kept it out. But there was no more than a moment to think about it. He too wanted to yell. He could cry out, rejoicing, because here it was finally, indisputably, as if a kind and merciful fairy had decided this poor bugger had suffered so much by now that he could be allowed a few minutes of pure pleasure.

The moist heat inside her was heaven itself. Smooth, warm flesh clasping equally smooth warm flesh. He got going with his hips, forced her open wider, the primal rocking of man in woman. Now he knew how meaningless all the previous times had been; a giant symphony had struck up in his balls and the echoes were rippling through his entire body.

Then his breath caught; she was clenching his penis with her pelvic muscles. A technique he had heard about but never experienced, he wondered where she had learnt it, with whom, and how much practice it had required. She let go, he thrust again, she clenched him again, warm flesh sucking him up and releasing him. To say it was incredibly stimulating was like calling the Empire State Building quite tall. And now there couldn't possibly be any doubt that she had wanted what was happening here just as much.

It was as he had imagined, but better – imagination could never conjure it *all* up. As he had pictured it, her skin was flawless, but in the dip between her left shoulder and breast was a small, sickle-shaped scar. It could have been the result of an accident, nothing serious, just enough to add the finishing touch and to announce: this is a *person* with an imperfection here and there.

They shared, gave and took wholeheartedly, with more and more honesty. And then it was time. He wanted to hold back, but even more, he wanted it immediately, because it had been building and building and postponing it was no longer possible. He wasn't just about to have an orgasm, it felt as if he was closer to exploding.

And then he was there, his mouth on hers, groaning, and feeling the world coming to an end.

21

The world got going again, although slowly. The two of them on this mess of a bed, her in the crook of his arm, body pressed tight against his.

Intimate, and relaxed.

When he'd been hoping for what had just happened, he hadn't thought beyond the physical act. Hadn't considered what would follow once they'd had sex. If he had hazarded a guess, he would have supposed she'd get dressed hastily, throw him an indecipherable look and leave. After which they would stick to the most basic conversation.

But her gaze was soft; her eyes revealed her feelings.

He thought this might well be called a state of euphoria, and it seemed to him she had gained a new dimension just as she had spirited something out of him.

Her warm breath caressed his cheek. 'I was afraid it would take weeks to get to this point.'

He laughed. 'I wasn't sure it ever would.'

'You should have more faith.'

Hmm, he thought, that's not exactly something I have left in spades.

But he kept it light. 'I don't even know you. Does that make me cheap?'

'Any girl with expensive taste knows cheap guys are the best.'

He laughed again. Heavens, she even had a sense of humour, yet another thing he hadn't seen much sign of until now.

And he was daft enough – he knew he was – to wonder if they could make this an almost daily occurrence. When Bernard had meetings in his study, she could come here, though they would have to be careful; it was just down the passage, after all. Or when Bernard was taking his afternoon naps. Or maybe he could take her to town. Her modest car was in the older of the two double garages, but she could say something was wrong with the engine and then they could drive to a secluded spot. Or …

In each scenario, however, it was Bernard who first had to be taken into account.

He found himself asking, 'How did it happen that—'

Michelle cut him short. 'Sometimes it's better not to know too much. Right now, you and me, we're just two people. But …' She raised her head and as he turned to look her in the eye, it was obvious that she decided he deserved an answer. 'Paul, if you're in my position, you need to think of where you're going.'

'Luckily you're a clever girl.'

'If I'm so clever, what am I doing here with you?' There it was again, that edge of humour to her voice.

And now, would he refer to it or not?

'When Bernard has money, you mean?'

There. It was out. He had tried to soften his voice to keep it from sounding critical but obviously didn't pull it off, because: 'You seem very judgemental. Someone like me has a short shelf life.' Her reply was cool, unlike the warmth of her body. 'The wheelchair does help.

Him not being able to get around. Literally not. Or that's at least how I reasoned until I realised I like him.'

'Is it?' He hadn't really wanted to hear this, but nevertheless it was oddly reassuring.

'Sometimes.'

'That's "like", not "love"?'

'Of course not. "Love", yes, sometimes.' She thought about it. 'I love him like a problem child.'

That wasn't the way Paul would have described him, but since his conscience was bothering him a wee bit about what had just taken place under Bernard's roof, he was possibly overly keen to see the man in a negative light. His own judgement was unreliable and she knew Bernard far, far better.

'What?' she encouraged. 'I can see you thinking. What are you thinking?'

'Not much.'

'Paul ... enough with the silences, please. Things are different now, don't you agree?'

Yes, Michelle, he wanted to say, everything has changed, but what now? And I still have a past, and God knows what happened in *yours*.

'It's still not easy for me to think of you being back in the problem child's bed tonight.'

'Men!' She waved a hand over her naked flesh. 'This is just a body.'

'But what a body.' With his arm still around her, he stroked across her stomach as far as he could reach. His cock was still at half-mast and was refusing to get the message that action was done with for the time being. 'Anyway, what's your full name?'

'Is this an inquisition?'

He was really coming to understand her, that's why he was so sure the laugh was hiding the fact that she was getting uncomfortable.

Even so, she told him. 'Michelle Beth Carlson. Happy?'

When she next spoke, a minute or so later, he knew she'd planned her words carefully. 'I wish I could make this moment last. But it's always the wrong ones that do ...'

'Hmm.'

'What are *you* wishing for?'

His turn to feel uncomfortable. Anything in the sphere of emotions and feelings is not the forte of many men, and even if he had been okay with this kind of thing, the What Happened had since screwed him up completely.

He tried to be honest. 'For ... a new beginning. Or I've known that for a long time, but it needs to be with the right person.' He gave her shoulder a gentle squeeze. 'And I wish I – we – could find the right place to start over.'

He couldn't believe he had said it so easily. And it had come out nicely, like words spoken by the hero in a romantic film. The kind of thing women always want men to say but only ever hear in movies.

'What is it you're trying so hard to escape, Paul?'

He couldn't stop himself. His body almost went rigid.

'Is it that obvious?'

'It's that obvious.' Michelle sat up a little to point at his open suitcase. 'You haven't unpacked. Look at that gigantic wardrobe, but there are your clothes, just as they were when you arrived.'

'I ... keep on moving.' He knew it was a weak explanation. 'Thanks to my severance package and the money I got for my old rust-bucket of a car, I can. I haven't unpacked it for almost six months.'

But now he was where he needed to be. Yet much as he wanted to enjoy every moment of holding her, the urge to share the events of that night was suddenly so strong that he began to talk.

'His name was Mike ...'

22

His name is Mike and you couldn't have asked for a better partner. When you, as one half of a team, often find yourself in rather unsavoury surroundings, it's essential that your partner is a) someone you get along with well and b) someone you can trust.

Sergeant Mike Wilkins. He has such a spontaneous nature that even that sourpuss Doris Black, the female police captain who never misses a chance to demonstrate to a man that she is more police captain than woman, sometimes allows herself a half-smile over something he says. But he isn't just a joker, and that's where the trust part comes in.

If he tells you he's going to do something, he'll do it. You'll never have to check. And if you land in a shit situation with him, you know he'll be watching your back.

And God have there been enough instances to test the truth of that! Everything the criminal minds of Pretoria could dish up. You have apprehended bank robbers, burglars, pickpockets, con artists and muggers and all-round evildoers, and those are merely the ones that are easily classifiable.

Over time, something strange happens. You don't respond the same way as you did in your first few years on the job, when violent situations were a good excuse to act however you wanted. It unfolded gradually, the hope that a few days would pass without violence. You started wondering if your aggressive tendencies had been satiated once and for all. Was that the case? You no longer try to spur perpetrators into aggression. Mike had something to do with that; unlike your previous partners, he stands for certain things about which you have always been cynical, but less so now that you have seen them in action.

He sets an example. It is surprising to wish you could be more like someone who is really too soft to be a policeman, who isn't even in shape and has one of the tiniest peckers you've ever seen on a fully grown man, but that's how it is.

And although you remain ready to be the one to hit the hardest when hitting really is called for, you no longer feel fine about it afterwards. But it has had the unfortunate consequence – it must have been the cause – of making you more and more tense. Since the possibility of danger will no longer offer a release, danger has become something you need to worry about.

Violence is no longer your friend, and at least once a week you throw up before leaving for work.

Thank God for Mike. He has arrived at the right time and without you knowing you needed him. When you get tense, he cracks a joke, or has the right words at the ready, or knows he should say nothing. Then it passes.

He has admitted that he sometimes gets just as worked up, but he obviously manages to approach it in the right way.

Mike Wilkins, thirty-year-old family man. Married just four years, and three kids already. Somehow he finds the time to give them and his wife enough attention, because they seem happy. They've had you over for supper a number of times, and you almost felt a pang of jealousy at the easy-going love you could feel throughout the house, but it's just right that it should be there for someone who gives so freely, whether it's a beer, or a chop, or moral support.

Still, the envy does bubble up when Isolde puts her arms around him and says something like 'Oh let me give you a cuddle, my old teddy bear!' You hope that one day you will experience the same kind of warmth and be able to handle it. But you don't begrudge Mike for it – who could be more deserving?

And he does look like a teddy bear, with his round face and mousy curls and a thinning crown. The incipient belly adds to the effect. A murderous exercise routine including a hundred daily sit-ups wouldn't undo the effects of a handful of bad habits: the sweets, the numerous Camel Lights, braaied meat with as much fat on as possible, the beers, the brandy and Cokes.

You will sometimes needle Mike about how well he is padded around the midriff, ask whether he'll have to buy yet another belt this month, and he will hit back with a comment about embittered bachelors. His favourite joke is 'Ten years ago I had the body of a Greek god, now I have the body of a Greek waiter!'

You realise that you exploit him at times. You've bent his ear about three of your 'relationships', and each time it turned into a much more exhausting conversation than you had planned. Father confessor, but in a relaxed way. He hasn't attempted to guide you in any direction, though some things might have been clearer to him than they were to you. And didn't make any remarks when you went for the next 'love'. Didn't give advice, either, though he must have been itching to. Too few people understand that even the world's best, or best-intentioned, advice is only welcome if it was requested.

You just had to talk, and to who else? He is your best friend.

You have realised he is your only friend, because you keep people at a distance. Now that everyone is no longer taking pains to avoid you, you feel as if you're itching on the inside as soon as your personal space is invaded. If you phone your mother and father more than once a month, they wonder what is wrong. Even then the conversation dries up after you've each enquired as to the other's health and the weather and spoken about any deaths in the immediate family. You inflicted too much damage all those years ago and in their silences you can hear their lack of trust. The house had already been quiet in the years before you were sent away; your parents' jobs demanded lots of time and sacrifice. It might have been different if you'd had a brother or sister.

Now you have a brother.

Mike Wilkins whistles softly beside you while you drive to the area where Alistair Bogart has been spotted.

Or might have been spotted. Officers never know how seriously to take tips of that kind. People imagine the most remarkable things to enjoy even a moment of attention.

Alistair Bogart, one of the most callous bastards Johannesburg has produced in years – and that is saying something. His MO? *Vicious attacks on couples in their home. He will tie up the man and have him watch his wife or girlfriend being tortured and raped before killing them both and walking away with whatever money he could lay his hands on. Which is often very little. As far as they can tell, there have been four such cases in Jo'burg.*

During what would have been the fifth double murder, things went wrong when the couple's neighbour went outside looking for his errant cat, heard a muffled scream and phoned the police. Bogart got away, shooting a constable dead in the process, but at least the perpetrator now had a name. By sheer coincidence the husband, who unlike his wife was still alive, had worked with Bogart in marketing and had bumped into him in a shop a few days earlier. Presumably, Bogart had followed him home from a distance.

It has been quiet the last two weeks. Now, if the caller's information is reliable, Bogart is in Pretoria.

'We'll see,' Mike says. 'The identikit wasn't up to much. My cousin looks like that. One of my school teachers, too. Hell, I look like that!'

That identikit has been on the front page of more than one daily newspaper. Soon enough there were calls to police stations around the country from people who were convinced they'd seen him. Each time, though, it turned out to not have been Alistair Bogart who was rude to the cashier at a McDonald's in Knysna, or who had been spotted near a school fence in Randfontein, or who had been begging on a corner near the Superspar in Sutherland.

You don't know why you are so bloody nervous. You try to hold your hands steady. Tonight it's as if you can sense every grain of evil hidden underneath the city's pretty disguise of lush jacarandas and well-kept lawns. Menace is around each corner; lying in wait, it will be upon you before you've had time to see it for what it is.

Mike crushes the filter of yet another Camel Light in the ashtray. The car always smells of dead smokes. You can tell he is uneasy from the way he holds his cigarettes.

Policemen and nervous wrecks – too often they are one and the same. You think of Fred Mapule, who took his own life when he couldn't face another day of heinousness and horrors, nor the shame of deserting his post. As if killing himself were a better option! You can clearly remember the day you walked into the station and heard the news. Fred's little boy had gone to the bathroom in the middle of the night and tripped over the upset chair before he noticed his daddy hanging from the ceiling.

How many stories there are ... but you've kept yourself in one piece by having eyes in the back of your head and not allowing things like that to get under your skin.

'It's two blocks further,' says Mike. Your stomach turns to a knot. While you knew you were that close, you didn't want to hear it.

You park around the corner; you will do the rest on foot.

Carefully. There are plenty of trees, which helps.

And there it is. Derelict, unlike the other houses. The neighbours must be distraught at how its appearance has devalued their property. The story behind such neglect? Who knows. Although the nearest streetlamp is dead, the moonlight shows how many broken windows there are, and that the front door is missing.

If the caller was right, Alistair Bogart is hiding inside. A woman living across the road has sworn he has the same face as on 'that made-up photo'. She only saw him briefly, but he 'acted so suspicious' when he went in.

That's no clear indication of the person in question being a criminal, because for years you've been well aware that the hugely wicked manage to behave like little angels when they want to.

You and Mike don't need to talk. To communicate with your partner you don't just use the gestures you learnt during training, you also develop your own private code, and six months is actually a very short time considering the degree to which you accomplished that. Now he trots ahead. You follow. He takes up position to the left of the door, you to the right.

You gesture to him to go around the back.

You are shit-scared, your mouth is dry, you want to turn and run. Or wait behind a tree. You can wait for Mike to walk through the house and then say you've also been inside and that there was nothing.

But you do what you have to do, and so you creep inside.

It isn't completely dark; you could tell from the outside that there would be enough moonlight coming through the broken windows. But that applies only to the rooms; not all that much finds its way into the passage down which you have to walk.

Maybe it's the place itself – that's what you are reacting to. Some places are just bad. But you'd got the feeling in the car.

You, with your right hand stretched out ahead. Your pistol searches the dark space in time with your eyes. A haunted house. You don't believe in that kind of thing, but this, surely, is how believers feel.

Hair on end and the skin on your neck crawling. The cold.

Ghosts can do nothing to you, but people can.

You can feel him here. It wasn't a false alarm. You wouldn't feel this way if there were no danger. Your palms are sweating. You'll have to watch out or you'll drop your weapon.

What is wrong with you? You should be used to this kind of thing. You were!

If Bogart is here, you and Mike will catch him, simple as that. His victims were people he caught unawares. They hadn't been armed. You two are.

Then, a crunch very close by. You swing the pistol wildly. Your breath comes loud, that and the crunch must have betrayed your position. You realise you've stepped on a piece of brick.

Get it together!

Time to move.

You can't.

But somehow you do. Ahead of you is a corner, a turn in the passage.

Where he could be waiting.

You get your breathing under control. Move as quietly as you can towards the first open door on the left. Is it the lounge? You assume so.

Another doorway diagonally opposite you. One a bit further down, on the opposite side, then another this side. And then the corner. But you pause, to orientate yourself. That's the excuse.

Remember, Mike will be coming towards you from that side, if he has entered right from the back. If he is already inside. He could have come in from the side, so don't scream if he suddenly appears.

He won't joke about it later if you do, but you'll think less of yourself.

You hold the pistol in front of you, police style. It was easy to learn; it was logical and it means you are ready. As far as your weapon is concerned, at least.

You still haven't even entered the first room. Goddammit, Paul!

You nearly have a heart attack when you squat down and look around the corner. You'd managed to suddenly convince yourself he would be only a metre or so away, that close, the kind of devil a child would imagine …

But no, the room, big enough to have been the lounge, is empty. Not only of people, also of furniture. Just bare wooden floorboards, drawings of cocks and cunts on the walls, other graffiti, moonlight playing with the shadows.

Back to the passage. You creep to the next door.

You establish that it's another empty room.

Why does the place have to be so damn big? There are so many rooms to hide in, it's ideal for someone like Bogart. If he is here … but he is, isn't he? How did he find the house? Did he already know of it, has he been looking around for a place, or did it attract him because it is equally malignant?

What the hell is taking Mike so long?

Maybe, if you simply stayed here … but no, you are in this thing together.

Another empty room.

And another. You survived them both.

The corner lies ahead. You would have thought it impossible, but now you are even more afraid. You thought you had the building plan all figured out, but all of a sudden you aren't sure that the passage really is going to take a left turn after this corner. It's become a bloody labyrinth. You are going to take that corner and be swallowed the way a python would a terrified animal, and there is no way back, you will … Stop it, fucking stop it!

'Mike?' It is madness, whispering. It's pure fucking crazy to do it,

but now you need to know where he is, you can't do this alone any longer ... 'Mike, where are you?'

You prick your ears, hoping for the sound of his voice, but you are equally scared that he will answer, because any sound will make you jump out of your skin now. But everything will be okay after that. Has to be, because it's only your thoughts scaring you, there's no one other than Mike here.

Silence.

'Dammit, Mike ...'

What will he think of you, if he hears you muttering when you are supposed to be completely silent? But he'll understand, he is Mike Wilkins.

You start to turn the corner and a figure rushes at you. No, it's your imagination playing more tricks, there's only darkness.

More doors to the left.

Labyrinth.

And ahead, another corner.

And.

Something has just disappeared around that corner.

A shape, a dark figure.

Except that it didn't happen. You saw it simply because you were expecting to.

Your heart refuses to quieten. You turn your head and try to listen. Now your ears are ringing. You have been holding your breath too long.

You move step by step, mustn't stumble on anything again.

If Mike came in, why haven't you found each other yet? The place isn't that big and you are already halfway in, or further.

Then, a sound.

Something falling.

A pistol on the floorboards, or some other solid object?

Whatever it is, it didn't fall of its own accord. The sound came from somewhere ahead, around the corner. It was Mike bumping into something, you try to convince yourself. He bumped into something and you stepped on a brick, both of you nice and clumsy tonight.

Otherwise … otherwise Mike might be in need of help.

You have to.

And so you do: take another step down the passage, and another, and another, because you are doing it for him. He is your partner and will do anything for you, and you are about to go around the corner.

You drop to your knees.

Peer around.

And again your subconscious produces a scene in which there is a devil.

This time, it remains unchanged for so long that it must be real. You'd expected some sort of surprise all along, but now that it's arrived you realise you weren't ready for it after all. Even though your heart has been beating so wildly and you got a fright over nothing again and again, the real danger brought with it an even worse feeling.

There is enough light to be able to see the man standing behind Mike, one arm clasped around his throat. He has a plain face, much like the one on the identikit, because the devil lives inside.

He has a gun pressed to Mike's head.

The pistol Mike dropped – the noise you heard – is lying a few paces away.

'Drop your weapon,' Bogart orders. He has a high-pitched voice, like a woman, and he sounds calm, even relaxed. 'Or I'll blow his brains away.'

You know you can't. It's all you have to use against him.

'Drop it. Now!'

But if you don't …

'Don't.' Mike has a hard time speaking the way he is being held. 'He's going to shoot anyway.'

'Shut. The. Fuck. Up.'

Words that are hissed. The sound of so much more evil than you ever had in yourself; here it is in its undiluted form.

Your legs are paralysed.

'Don't, Paul!'

'Do it now,' orders the man, his face behind Mike's shoulder.

You have to make a decision. You make it.

It will have to be quick. You hold your pistol as tight as your clammy palm allows, raise it, curl your finger around the trigger and pull.

The shot. The recoil in your arm.

Something jerks where the two men are standing together as one.

First echo. It is so loud, all around you, that you almost think it's a second shot. The shock courses through you even though you can't believe what you are seeing.

Second echo. You have to believe it now: a dark spot on Mike's forehead, his mouth half-open, his wide eyes, and the surprise in them.

The man lets go. Mike's body hits the floor and stays lying there, a discarded teddy bear.

The man slips away and becomes one with the darkness. You can't stop him. Your hand holding the pistol is hanging at your side. The echoes are long gone. Everything is quiet apart from the sounds you are making.

23

'The guy might have let Mike go,' he heard himself say. 'Then everything would have been all right.'

Her body was still soft beside his. Had he really shared all that with her? The only person with whom he'd discussed it in such detail had been the police counsellor.

'Paul ...'

Michelle's face spoke of sympathy – but not pity, thank God.

'It was me. It was *me*.'

'He wouldn't have let him go. You know that.'

'I don't.'

'It's a terrible thing to have happened.' She pulled him even closer, held him. In a world where nothing helped, *this* did. 'No one would expect you to get over it quickly.'

He realised his cheeks were wet. 'I couldn't touch one again. A gun. It's a murder weapon.'

'You shouldn't feel—'

'And to think I was one of the best when it came to shooting. What use is a policeman if he can't even draw his weapon? I just had to get away.'

Any time he as much as saw a pistol, he felt like throwing up. It put him right back in that moment, just the way he still got caught up in it every night. And the irony!

In the end it wasn't Alistair Bogart who'd been the dangerous one: it was *him*. Him who'd shot and killed Mike. The real devil had a completely different face.

To add to this, Bogart died two days later after being hit by a car as he was crossing a highway. Fate already had him booked; the outcome would have been the same whether or not two policemen had approached his hideout.

'Getting away,' Michelle whispered. He could hear her thoughts taking their own course. 'To be able to keep getting away, you need money. Plenty of it.'

Money doesn't help, he wanted to say, but then there was a noise and both of them turned their heads towards the door.

'Oh fuck,' he whispered.

Someone was poking at the keyhole.

They jumped up, grabbed their clothes. Paul dropped his pants, grabbed them again. Michelle looked around wildly – it appeared she was planning to slip underneath the bed, because it was high enough, but he pointed at the wardrobe. It was big … and empty.

He pulled open the door and was relieved that the hinges were silent.

He let her in before he squeezed in after her. Was the bedroom door opening yet? He couldn't look behind him, had to get into the wardrobe, into a space that turned out to be significantly more cramped than he had envisaged, seeing as it hadn't exactly been designed to hide a pair of full-grown adults. He had to push up against Michelle with all his might, but didn't want to force her into the back of the thing. But there was no time for niceties.

Somehow he did it. He angled himself to allow her to stand beside him instead of behind him, slightly hunched, with her head pressed up against the shelf space above her. Clutching his clothes and shoes like she was clutching hers, he swiftly pulled the door shut.

It wasn't as dark as he had expected. The shutters. He had a slatted view of the room.

And of the door opening.

Michelle's breath was on his torso. He could hear she was trying to keep it down.

Johnny entered the room cautiously. Looked around. Hastily closed the door behind him.

Motherfucker, thought Paul.

In Johnny's hand was the sharp object – a small file? – he must have used to open the lock. He slipped it into his back pocket.

He decided to do this in the dining room, Paul realised. When I said I was going for a walk, he knew it would be a safe time to snoop around. Had probably been wanting to do it for ages.

Then Paul froze inside, as he remembered the key.

In his mind's eye he saw it fall to the floor as he locked the door after Michelle arrived. How it had stayed on the floorboards.

Where Johnny could step on it.

Had it stayed in the lock, Johnny wouldn't have been able to open the door and probably wouldn't have been able to understand what was wrong. He would have left, and they wouldn't have been in this cock-up.

Johnny looked straight ahead. The key couldn't have been more than a ruler's width from his shoe.

He walked further in, and the key lay behind him, unnoticed.

Paul started to breathe through his teeth, so angry he wanted to hiss, and he might have, but Michelle had wriggled her hand from between them and pressed it to his mouth.

He became aware of another feeling. He shouldn't have been that anxious, but *she* was, and she was passing it on. If they were discovered there, he would be able to walk away with some regret, but also with the memory of the best sex he'd ever had. And her? She had reason to be afraid. *Someone like me has a short shelf life.* Girls like her might never come upon a golden goose like Bernard Russell again. Johnny would be falling all over himself to get the news to his employer, with the necessary regret in his voice while his eyes would be twinkling.

Then Paul realised he wasn't feeling anxious merely because the woman beside him felt it so keenly. In the time since What Happened, he had managed to get worked up over plenty of insignificant things – the nightly punishment had contributed to his overreactions to impulse. When the counsellor had told him he had post-traumatic stress, he'd wanted to punch her for glibly ascribing his unique form of torture to a disorder that afflicted so many others.

Johnny had found the open suitcase. He fished around in the clothes with care, wanting to leave it looking undisturbed.

What was he looking for? Paul believed anything would do, and he also knew why this search was being conducted. A man like Johnny, who was likely hiding more things than the average family put together, had recognised another carrier of secrets and wanted to find a stick with which to beat him off. Then he would be back in the post that had offered him so much more prestige than his current one.

There was a look of dissatisfaction on his sharp face when the suitcase failed to offer up any great revelations, only an unsurprising blend of underwear, socks and shirts. The meerkat-being went in for a deeper scratch, but stood back, empty-pawed.

His head swung on its thin neck as he looked around and Paul could hear him thinking: Where next?

The answer showed on his face.

The wardrobe.

He took the first step towards it ... and them.

Paul felt Michelle stiffen. His body reacted the same way. One, two, three paces. From behind the louvred doors, Paul saw Johnny looming larger, taking one step, then another. And then he was upon them, his face as close as if they were in conversation.

Next he would open the door.

It stayed closed.

Johnny had whipped around. It was his turn to look at the bedroom door, shoulders tight.

There was a sound coming from outside. Scratching, as when Johnny was trying to get in, but this one was louder because the person wasn't working at the lock with a file; this was a key being inserted into the keyhole.

Johnny dived to the floor and rolled underneath the bed. At the end of this smooth move the bedding caught his shoe, exposing the end of the bed.

Paul heard Michelle suck in her breath at the same moment that he saw it: black on white. Just a slip of it, but black on white. Was it her bra or her panties?

The bra. He remembered how it had fallen away when he'd undone it.

The door opened and Mary walked in. She gave the door a look, her frown deep as usual; Paul knew she had expected it to be locked, which was why she had used the key. She had to be surprised that the visitor who gave so little away about himself hadn't done so.

The key. It had been a stroke of grace for Johnny to miss it, but for Mary to overlook it as well, that would be too much to hope for.

In one hand she held a bunch of keys, in the other a vase of fresh flowers. More white roses. She marched to the desk – *without* seeing what was lying on the ground – and picked up the old vase, replacing it with the new.

Not safe yet. There was still the bed.

Mary turned around and saw how untidy it was.

That was all she saw, Paul realised, when she clicked her tongue. Not the bra. It was just a slip of black lace, only visible from where he was.

But she was heading for the bed. *Now* she'd see. How could he explain away the presence of lingerie in his room? She might even recognise it, and if not, certainly draw her own conclusions and take the news straight to Bernard.

Paul thought about Johnny underneath the bed. How close to the edge was he? He supposed he was able to see her feet.

Mary grabbed hold of the bedding.

Whipped it up so it covered more of the bed.

Covering up the bra.

She turned towards the door, and the key – that miserable key lying on the floor, which could lead her to suspect that the door had been locked from the inside and that the room was not as empty as it appeared – but again she missed it, as if guided by angels or destiny.

Angels. Guardian angels. Today they were working overtime.

She closed the door behind her.

Johnny rolled out from under the bed, pale. He got up, rushed over to the door ... and stopped suddenly.

This time he had seen it, Paul knew he had.

But Johnny didn't look down. He had his ear pressed up against the wood.

Paul allowed himself to relax a bit. Even though Johnny was in a hurry to get out of there, he was most likely waiting to be sure Mary was gone.

A few seconds more and he slipped out. The door closed.

Paul exhaled so loudly that he didn't hear Michelle do the same, he just felt the rush of heat on his arm. The absurdity of the last few minutes hit him and he wanted to laugh. *Two* threats, but both people had come and gone without incident!

Michelle's hand was back on his shoulder and he heard something hit the bottom of the wardrobe; her shoes and clothes. He half-turned and the dusky light revealed the impenetrable expression on her face. He was trying to figure it out when she put out her hand and stroked his chest.

'And now?' he asked. 'You look ...'

Her eyes were close enough for him to note the effect the situation had had on her. The enforced closeness, the danger of being discovered. She brought her lips to his ear and whispered as if there were still someone in the room.

'Have you ever done it in a closet?'

24

Judging by the smell of meat and spice that pervaded the kitchen and its surroundings, lunch wasn't going to be a mean affair. Mary was instructing Johnny how to cut the meat into cubes *just* like this – no bigger, no smaller.

Paul was happy with the picture he saw as he sauntered past the open door as if by pure coincidence. Johnny would be occupied a good while, and so would Mary. As for the rest of the house, silence reigned. Michelle had gone to check up on Bernard and Lindsey was nowhere to be seen.

No witnesses.

Unlike Johnny, he didn't use a file. The method of inserting a length of wire into a keyhole to tease open the lock wasn't something he had learnt in the police, but at school, during his short-lived friendship with an equally no-good named Jaque. Odd that he couldn't remember Jaque's surname, only that, unlike the distinctively spelt first name, it was an ordinary one spelt the ordinary way. Funny how some things you think you'll remember forever just disappear; and other moments you don't consider remarkable, they *stay*.

Now, just as when he'd graduated in this activity under the watchful eye of his instructor, the lock surrendered like a virgin at the touch of an experienced hand. Paul slipped in and closed the door.

So, this was Johnny's room.

And when Johnny came back later and found the door unlocked, he would think he had forgotten to lock it. You could count on most people to make things easier for criminals by being inattentive or by ascribing small but important discrepancies to their own absent-mindedness.

Paul looked around. Even a sergeant major would have had to concede the bed was neatly made. Nothing was untidy, nothing appeared to have been mindlessly plonked down. The smell of Johnny's cigarettes lingered despite the open window. It was blended with something more pleasant: on a desk that looked just like the one in his own room there was a vase. It contained just two roses; he had received three, but perhaps that hadn't been a deliberate act.

What was he looking for? Difficult to say, but Johnny wasn't the only one who could play this game.

The contents of his cupboards were a disappointment. Shirts folded, pants on clothes hangers. Not a lot of clothes, but no cheap materials. A cheap guy with expensive taste, in other words. There was only one pair of shoes other than the pair on Johnny's feet, and they were also polished. His socks harboured no holes. He coddled his crown jewels in Jockeys.

Paul knew he shouldn't feel disappointed. After all, it wasn't like he'd been expecting bricks of heroin or pictures of naked children.

No hidey holes in this room, and no loose floorboards.

But he wasn't done yet. The nightstand.

The drawer was just about empty. Only two packs of Chesterfield and a bronze lighter … and the item he had been hoping to find.

He took out the ID book and opened it. Unmistakable, the jagged features with the chin somewhat raised. The hair was brushed flat, choirboy style, but the expression was partly defensive, partly aggressive. As if the photographer had just called John Phillip Dunne a wanker.

25

He could have done it from his room, but he wanted to get out into the sun. And put some distance between himself and the house before he called.

He keyed in the number as he reached the first vines, the scent of grapes enveloping him like heavy perfume.

'Paul Mullan?' Her voice was coming all the way from Pretoria, but it was as clear as if she were standing next to him. 'Is it really you?'

'It's me.' He laughed.

'I thought I was just seeing what I wanted to see on this little screen.'

Always so forthright.

'Are you well, Sandra?'

He had some nerve calling her, even though he could tell she wasn't bearing a grudge. Which made it worse. Long before What Happened, even, he wasn't relationship material. And that remains what most women hope for – a relationship that will quickly lead to marriage. If only their expectations weren't so different to men's.

And didn't she just.

And then Candice was the one he took away to the spa.

Of course, it was a fantastic weekend.

Somewhere in the back of his mind he knew it was all about the novelty, and there was some measure of guilt, especially when he started suspecting that Sandra had realised something had changed between them. The warmth simply wasn't enough anymore. Nor were the little things: the fact that she'd darn his socks without any fuss, or sew a button onto his shirt. What he was after now was what Candice sounded like in the heat of her multiple orgasms.

And then Candice stopped answering his calls. Didn't return them.

Eventually, just an SMS:

Husband back sorry

Shit. A husband? And where had *he* been the whole time?

'You're messing Sandra around.' Mike broke his rule of not passing comment one afternoon for a sermon of scarcely more than five seconds, and it was clear that Sandra had spoken to him. 'You need to treat her better, or you need to let her go so she can get on with her life.'

Let her go? Then he'd have to start looking all over again. So he decided to treat her to a weekend away and to tell her he'd been feeling off for a while but that he was all better now. Some women will always expect the problem to have been their own doing anyway.

'Are you still there?' her voice suddenly reached him again.

And Paul was back in the most breathtaking valley imaginable, surrounded by vineyards. How he missed those days when he thought he had problems!

'Yup. Sandra, I need a favour ...'

'Izzit? I thought so.'

'It's a guy.'

'Shoot.'

'Someone I'm curious about,' he explained without knowing why he felt he needed to justify himself, maybe so that she would have less reason to think badly of him. 'Someone who wants to know more about me than he needs to, which has made me wonder about *him*. So I wondered if you could take a look at the system, to see if there's anything on him.'

'Name.'

'John Phillip Dunne. Phillip with two Ls, D-u-n-n-e.'

He heard the clicks on the keyboard. He could picture her behind the counter as uniformed colleagues passed by. There was always the smell of Ricoffy, and he wondered how many cups she had had that morning. Was her hair longer, or was she keeping it short? Blonde. It had helped that she was blonde.

While Michelle's is dark. Yes, now there's Michelle ...

Sandra had been overjoyed when they got to the spa. 'Are you sure you can you afford it?' she cried. She couldn't get enough of looking around, and she wanted to touch everything. 'You must let me pay half, absolutely!'

'Nonsense.'

It was great. Even better than the weekend he had spent there with Candice, because he realised being at ease counted for more. He could be himself with Sandra, without the pressure of having to act like Mr Sex God all the time, as he had wanted to for Candice.

But then on the Sunday morning a cleaner arrived and spoilt everything. She hadn't been there the day before, but after he and Sandra had shared a delightful breakfast, they found her in the room, making the bed.

'Ah, you're back, sir!'

'No, I've never been here before,' Paul tried.

'But sir!' Chatty type. 'I made the room that time.'

'I think you're confusing me with someone else.' He tried to signal with his eyes, conscious of Sandra right behind him.

'Oh, but you were in this same room, and the missus, her hair was just a little longer, with more curls …'

Then realisation dawned.

She left quickly, without finishing the suite.

It was weeks before Sandra spoke to him again. And then it was to say that she was so sorry about What Happened, was there something she could do to help?

Today, again, there was regret in her voice. 'I'm afraid not. Nothing on your John Phillip Dunne. So either he's clean, or he hasn't been caught yet.'

'Dammit, but thanks for trying. Oh, but wait. Another thing.'

Because it would be stupid not to.

'What?' Sandra asked.

'If you could look up someone else for me …'

26

'This food tastes better than Mary's.' Lindsey leaned over, whispering. 'If I didn't feel so sorry for Johnny I'd wish he could be in the kitchen permanently!'

'Tastes good, yes.' Paul took a bite of the goulash and didn't correct her – if she didn't know that Mary was still in complete control of whatever made it onto the plate, he wasn't about to enlighten her.

Besides, his attention was focused on the other side of the table.

Michelle was eating serenely. She looked positively demure. It was difficult to stop himself from staring. He wanted to touch her even more badly than before, because now he knew what it would feel like. The smooth skin, the heat from within, the firmness. He was going to go off his head with her around day in and day out, with the two of them being able to give each other just enough attention to not come across as unseemly.

Then there was a sound from the stairway. The stairlift was coming down.

'Don't.' Lindsey tried to stop him from getting up. 'He always wants to manage it by himself.'

So Paul stayed seated, and the three of them continued eating.

There was a muted groan from the stairs, the sound of metal, of wheels turning over wood and going quiet as they reached the carpet.

Mary must have been in the hallway, because she pushed the wheelchair into the room.

'I thought I heard you coming.' Michelle smiled at Bernard.

'It takes more than a migraine to keep me down.'

Mary parked the wheelchair at the head of the table. 'I'll bring Mister Bernard's plate.' To which she shouldered the swing door in a fashion that many a Springbok could only hope to equal.

Bernard swept his arm over the table in a grandiose arc. 'So, what's been happening? What did I miss?'

A woman taking a man by the hand and leading him to bed, the two of them hurling themselves onto said bed, the tearing off of clothes, his hands on her breasts, her hands on his erection, him entering her, the way she cried out.

Those were the thoughts running through Paul's head. *That's* what you missed, Bernard.

'I'm glad you're feeling better, Dad,' said Lindsey. 'I'm going to town soon. Just tell me if you need me to bring something back.'

'As if they could stock anything we don't already have!'

Go on, boast, thought Paul. You think you have everything. You don't.

To hell with feeling bad about what happened. And what was going to happen again. The regret would never be any match for the pleasure and satisfaction.

'Just say if you need me to take you,' he offered.

Lindsey blushed slightly. 'But you aren't *my* chauffeur.'

'He can take you if you'd like,' said Bernard.

'That's okay. Thanks, Paul. I'm fine.'

Michelle looked over at Bernard. 'I'm glad you feel better too.'

'Oh, really?'

It might have been a pointed question, but not paired with that look of appreciation. Paul wondered how much this man had grown to depend on her.

'Yes, really.'

She was such a good actress – and as this thought crossed Paul's mind, he heard Sandra's voice again, after she had entered the second name in the crime register:

With her I can help. She's been a busy girl, your Michelle Beth Carlson.

It wasn't a betrayal, he tried to convince himself, because when he had asked Michelle her full name up there in bed, he had really just wanted to get to know her better, without this kind of purpose in mind.

On record for housebreaking. Drugs, that was the reason. She wanted money.

It was hard to believe that the woman opposite him had ever been in the clutches of drugs. Not this creature reaching for Bernard with an elegant hand, surely not.

After which she had a boyfriend. An older man, a 'mentor'. He took care of her financially.

Bernard's hand met hers.

Until the day he went off the side of a cliff. Purportedly suicide when she left him after the money ran out.

Bernard gave her hand a squeeze.

Since then, nothing. Why do you want to know about her?

Because I'm crazy about her.

Her, holding another man's hand.

He couldn't remember what he had told Sandra.

He tried not to think about what it could be like when Bernard and Michelle went to bed, and the ways in which it might differ from just hours ago when he and she had …

He was the fresh arrival. The status quo had been sorted. He had nothing to offer her, or at least not the earthly possessions this older man could give her. He'd have to get used to it or get lost. When you're obsessed with a woman, you cancel all your options.

'You're so quiet, Paul,' Lindsey remarked.

'Am I?'

He put on a disarming look and chatted along, laughed at one of Bernard's little jokes, and the time passed after all. It had become easier towards the end.

Michelle went upstairs with Bernard and about fifteen minutes later Paul glanced out the front door. Lindsey was driving off in a blue Aygo.

A bigger car wouldn't have suited her, he thought. She drove slowly, as if she was worried the gravel might hurt the car.

'Sometimes I worry about that child.'

The voice came from behind him. For a moment he couldn't believe it was Mary. But the concern was there, along with that severe frown. She was far more nuanced than he had given her credit for, although it had long been clear from the way she treated Bernard.

'She looks like she can take care of herself.'

'Some girls need someone. And her father is busy. Always.'

Well, well, well. Was that a hint of criticism?

'I suppose he needs to keep making money.'

Mary laughed. It was the first time he had heard her laugh.

'Don't think I haven't noticed the way you two look at each other.'

'You can see anything if you put enough imagination into it,' he protested.

Even so, he was relieved. If Mary wanted to believe she had seen something between him and Lindsey, it meant she wouldn't develop any suspicions about him and Michelle. From Lindsey's side the interest remained obvious, or in any case it was to him, so either she wasn't artful enough to hide it or she had decided the best approach was to let it show.

'I might not have minded.' The stern tone was back in Mary's voice. 'It could do Lindsey good, the attention. If I could only be sure.'

'Sure of what?'

She grunted because he needed to ask. 'That it isn't all about money for you, too.'

And with that she walked away. Paul watched her go, a frown on his own face now.

Then he saw Johnny go past, giving him an enquiring look.

He recalled what Michelle had said the previous day: *There are eyes and ears wherever you turn, aren't there?*

27

It was a lovely afternoon, and at times lovely days followed on so uninterruptedly in the area that for some of the residents they later on hardly even registered. Given the rich spectacle of golden-green fields and indigo mountains, too many days of sunshine could easily lead to satiation. But in periods when the weather was so changeable, as it was now, they could be appreciated more wholeheartedly.

Lindsey had pulled the seat right forward and was sitting almost on the edge. She always drove that way. It made it easier for her to see over the steering wheel.

What she saw now that she had turned off was the panorama just before you got into town: the mountain to the left, dipping gently, with a bigger piece of mountain behind, and the two lines meeting right over the white line on the road. There were neat vineyards on either side of the road, guiding the eye to small dwellings that from the outside appeared completely unchanged over centuries, enveloped in a profusion of trees.

She drove along, as always, up Van Riebeeck Street, right into Skool and up the hill into Kerk.

All was well. The only sound was the engine of the blue Aygo.

And then on to her parking spot, close to the hotel.

The car, the road, the silence, the town. Nothing looked out of place.

So much can change in a matter of moments.

28

Paul was coming around the corner of the house when he heard the cry.

Like a wounded animal.

Pain and fury.

The day was too beautiful to spend indoors and he had wanted to stretch his legs again. As big as his bedroom was, the walls started to close in on him when he spent too long in there, and even though he and Michelle had been in that bed together, it was still the place where the nightmare came for him, and he was due for another visit.

And who could he sit around with and engage in chit-chat? Lindsey, when she got back from town? Mary already had it in her head that something was up between them, and he didn't want Bernard on his case too, should he cotton on to the same idea.

He'd made his way past the tree, noticing how it looked utterly impossible for someone in dress shoes to get up there. Past the two double garages, one with much rougher walls than the other, seemingly built when the original no longer sufficed, the yard from which Mary's chickens gave him reproachful looks, a veggie patch, flowerbeds, the window of what turned out to be a storeroom, through which he could see the angular lines of furniture under sheets, and the window that looked into the pantry.

One of the windows at the back of the house might belong to Mary's room; he didn't know which, because there were two with the curtains drawn.

It was then that he heard the noise. He turned around to look at the open window above, Bernard and Michelle's.

It wasn't *her*.

Paul burst inside and ran through the hallway, nearly colliding with Johnny, also on his way to the stairs.

There was another roar of pain and anger once they were almost upstairs.

Paul threw open the bedroom door and saw Michelle hunched over Bernard, who was sitting in his wheelchair a few paces from the bed. She was clearly trying to calm him.

'What's going on?' Paul asked.

Johnny was beside him. 'Bernard?'

'Something terrible has happened.' Michelle looked terrified. 'Lindsey has been—'

'I can talk for myself!' Bernard interrupted her. 'My child ...' He was fighting back the emotion, his face red, the robust voice faint as if his throat was being squeezed. 'She's been taken.'

'What? Lindsey taken?' cried Mary, who had just appeared.

'They called a minute ago.' Bernard threw the cell phone down in his lap, but it slid off and landed on the Persian carpet. 'A man. He says we'll find Lindsey's car near the hotel, with her keys inside. We can simply go pick it up. But it will cost more to get *her* back.'

Michelle looked as if she was thinking of moving back towards Bernard, but decided it was wiser to stay put.

Someone has to take control, thought Paul. And that had been his job: people in crisis. Even though that was no longer his life, he had no other choice now.

'It wasn't anyone you know?'

Bernard glared at him. 'It was a man, I said. I would have said who if I knew!' He tried to get a hold of himself. 'Sorry. I ... No.'

'What kind of voice?'

'What do you mean?'

'White man, black man?'

'It ... kind of sounded like a black man. But maybe it wasn't.'

Paul frowned. 'Why not?'

'There are things people can do to disguise their voices.'

'But that kind of thing doesn't make you sound different in *that* way.'

'I don't think it was a black man!' Bernard was close to exploding again. 'What does it matter, anyway?'

'Did he say what it would cost you?'

'Three point two million.'

'Three point two million!' Mary cried from behind Paul.

Now she was the one facing a glare.

'Do you think I don't *have* it? I just want my child back!'

Paul found it unreal, seeing the man like this. The figure that had filled the wheelchair so completely seemed smaller, hunched. Only his fury was enormous, like an emergency generator that would be able to supply power for quite some time.

'We need to call the police,' said Johnny.

'You can bloody forget about that!'

'Did he tell you not to?'

'He didn't have to tell me. One knows these things!'

Michelle moved closer after all. 'Bernard ...'

'I will *not* call them. We'll do,' and he swallowed, 'we'll do just what he says. What they say. He spoke about "we".'

'That means nothing,' said Paul. 'If there's just one, he'll usually make it sound as if there are at least a handful. At least you've already heard from him – or from them. Lindsey isn't simply missing. You know what's happening. And if you don't want to involve the police—'

'I don't want to! I've told you!'

'Lindsey is gone,' Mary said, sounding defeated. 'But she just drove off here like always?'

'Let me guess.' Paul picked up the cell phone and handed it to Bernard. 'There was no caller ID and you can't call back. They'll have a throwaway cell, or more than one.' He gave the others a quick glance, because he felt it was time to explain. 'I'm a policeman. Was a policeman.'

'Is there anyone here who didn't know that?' Johnny was so easy to read. Pissed off because his suggestion of calling the police had been rejected and someone else was able to take the lead.

Paul ignored him. 'Bernard, you said you have the money. And you're prepared to pay. If the person gets it, he'll have no reason to harm her. If he's a pro, and it sounds like it, he would have made sure Lindsey didn't see his face so that she wouldn't be able to ID him later. That means she's no danger to him. Did he say how he wanted it handed over?'

'He said he'd call again.' The fire on the man's cheeks had started fading, and it seemed the fury would subside along with it. Soon it would turn to shock, Paul knew. 'He said I'd have to give the matter some thought first.'

'It's a mind game, remember that.'

'The bastard knows I'll play along! Further instructions to follow, he said. But yes.' Bernard hesitated. 'He *did* say how.'

'And ...?'

'That you have to take it.'

'Me?'

'Yes, I was looking at you, wasn't I?' Bernard closed his eyes again. 'Sorry. Yes, you.'

'So he knows about me.' Now they're going to start suspecting me, thought Paul. He would have, too, if he were in their shoes. Even to him it sounded unconvincing when he said, 'But I suppose he knows about everyone around here.'

Johnny sniffed.

'He knows about *everyone*, yes.' Bernard took Michelle's hand and gave it a little squeeze. 'You have to go too, my girl. You have to carry the briefcase.'

Her dark eyes, filled with support for him just moments ago, flew wide open.

29

He and Johnny drove to Riebeek-Kasteel to collect Lindsey's car. It felt beyond odd to sit at the wheel in Johnny's uniform with Johnny in the passenger seat, but who could ever guess what any given day might hold?

At lunchtime Lindsey was on the farm, and now God knows where she might be.

At breakfast he and Michelle had yet to explore each other physically.

If you want your circumstances to change in the blink of an eye, come to the Boland. Paul recalled the premonition he'd had. Oh, for hindsight. Clearly his radar was set on trouble. Mishap and guilt weren't enough, and for too long there had been no new problems.

'Hmph, this is quite something,' remarked Johnny.

Paul didn't react. And it didn't sound as if the guy expected him to. Some people were destined never to become friends. Even if the entire household was kidnapped, he knew he and Johnny would remain at loggerheads. Just to have the man sitting there, breathing, was enough to make the palm of his smacking hand itch.

Abduction ... a melodramatic word that seemed coined for adventure stories. Lindsey had been taken. Nabbed. But it remained abduction.

Johnny's jaw had been working at a piece of gum long before they'd left home, but traces of smoke were still there when he spoke, or exhaled strongly, the same way it clung to his clothes and hair. The gum was peppermint flavoured, which he clearly believed righted everything; Paul, however, thought it was like someone spritzing a little potpourri-scented spray after taking a really foul dump and thinking it was all that was needed to turn the toilet into an inviting haven for the next occupant. And what would the next occupant smell? Not potpourri. Shit sprinkled with a little potpourri.

Reaching town, Paul followed the same route he had taken when driving Bernard and Michelle to the restaurant. The hotel was just a few metres further down the road.

The blue Aygo was empty and there was not a soul in sight. Paul knew there wouldn't be much point in asking around; especially in such a quiet spot, the odds were around a hundred to one that no one would have seen a thing. He'd had plenty of experience of that. Anyway, Bernard had forbidden them to do so.

He parked the Mercedes near the Aygo and turned off the engine.

He and Mike doing their rounds – suddenly those were the images flooding his mind. Mike exhaling his smoke through the car window. Mike laughing, his round face, the teddy-bear man. Chewing gum worked on *him*.

Forget it, he thought. Or at least for now. You can let it out again tonight, but you're with another guy now. And you're not doing the rounds, you're here for a completely different reason.

He and Johnny got out and walked over to the Aygo, where Paul peered through the tinted window on the driver's side.

'There are the keys, on the floor.'

The door was unlocked. He opened it and bent over to retrieve the keys. The car's interior was warm from being closed up for a long time, and now that the late-afternoon chill was setting in it was actually pretty cosy.

How had it happened? Lindsey parked here, and *then*?

Or had she been somewhere else, and someone forced her to ...?

No. Paul reckoned she had parked here herself. And then something had happened. They – or he – might have been waiting for the right opportunity, waited close to the farm for a while, following Lindsey from there, knowing the right moment had come when they saw her park with nobody around.

And then? A handkerchief with chloroform? A pistol against her head, or partially covered with a jacket and pressed into her side so that she had no option but to do what they said?

Peaceful surroundings. People were getting ready to eat supper.

He considered walking into the hotel after all and asking whether anyone had seen anything, but had to respect Bernard's wishes. In any case, if someone had noticed anything, he or she would have likely come out by now, what with them standing around the car.

He gave Johnny the keys. 'You can drive it back.'

'Oh, is that what you've decided?'

'That's what I've decided.'

They left town via Hermon Street and turned right, back to the farm, Johnny staying behind Paul for a while. The road was quiet, but of course Johnny had to overtake the Mercedes right when there was an oncoming truck.

The blaring horn conveyed the driver's discontent and a middle finger appeared from the Aygo's open window. John Phillip Dunne in a nutshell.

But he was right in one regard, thought Paul. This business with Lindsey, it really was quite something.

30

According to the stinkwood grandfather clock in the corner, it was nineteen minutes past eight, but to Paul it felt much later.

The same was true for Bernard. He could tell. The man was gazing into the red and yellow flames of the hearth, his hand on a half-empty brandy glass. Apart from a tightly set jaw, his face didn't give much away, but tension was written all over his upper body.

Michelle sat reading a magazine, but the listless way she turned a page every few minutes showed him she wasn't absorbing much.

It was just the three of them, because more than an hour ago Johnny had announced he was setting off for Malmesbury to see a friend.

Last night there had been six of them under this roof ...

Paul could still see Lindsey sitting there, head tilted when she spoke, her particular smile, with a touch of sadness beneath the cheer. But maybe it was hindsight that made him see that aspect. Whatever the case, that softness of hers had made her grow on him quickly.

Sometimes I worry about that child, Mary had said, and there had been reason for concern, albeit from an angle they'd never have considered.

Initially, some people might judge her. Rich kid. Privileged and spoilt. But this would change after a few minutes in her company. Add to that the fact that her mother had died just four months earlier, and in *that* way, and that her father tumbled down the bloody stairs a month later … well, Lindsey certainly didn't deserve this too. What's more, Bernard most likely had a troublesome temperament throughout her childhood, and it would have intensified after the accident.

Where was she now? How scared would she be, far away from familiar faces and the restorative atmosphere of flames in a hearth?

The long hand on the grandfather clock was still moving, the pendulum driving the ticking, but each minute felt longer than the one before.

Even so, eventually it was quarter to nine.

'It could drive a person mad.' Bernard looked at the empty glass he had brought to his lips.

The swing doors opened and Mary walked in briskly, but then stopped in her tracks.

'Oh.'

'Come in, Mary.' Bernard pointed at the liquor cabinet with his free hand. 'Help yourself.'

'I didn't know you and the others were still down here, Mister Bernard.'

'We're not ready for bed yet.'

'What a thing to happen, sir.'

Bernard looked at Paul. 'Mary doesn't drink, but …'

'I should *think* I don't drink, Mister Bernard.'

'But I've managed to convince her to take one of these every evening. It helps one sleep well.'

'Tonight I also need something like that.' Michelle took another sip of red wine.

Mary looked self-conscious as she walked over to the liquor cabinet and poured her brandy. As if it were a chink in her armour she hadn't wanted to show.

'And for you, sir?'

'I think so.' Bernard held out his glass.

No offer from Mary's side to do the same for Paul or Michelle.

Then she walked away with a 'Night, sir' and a nod at Paul. You might easily have thought she hadn't seen Michelle at all.

Silence.

Just the ticking.

The long wait.

Another tick.

Bernard looked at the cell phone on his lap again. Took a sip from his glass, swirled the brandy around his mouth, swallowed it.

'You know, it's odd that you got here just before … you know.'

'There was no time for me to have been able to organise anything,' Paul protested. 'Or there might have been, but you know it was sheer coincidence that you and Johnny picked me up from the side of the road—'

'No, man!' Bernard shook his head. 'What I mean … I'm glad there's someone around here who can go over there. Wherever that might be. When they call again. Because Johnny wouldn't have been able to handle it.'

'I get that,' Michelle said.

'I'm sorry you've been dragged into this. I hadn't even asked you if you'd go.'

'In for a penny, in for three point two million rand?'

That reminded him. 'There's something I still want to ask you, Bernard.'

That was as subtle as he could be to find out whether he was free to talk in Michelle's presence.

'Anything Michelle gets to hear, she can hear,' said Bernard.

'Right then. Three point two million rand is a very specific amount.'

'Yes.'

'Why not just three million? Or three point five?'

Bernard hesitated, then set his glass down on the side table and swung the wheelchair around.

'Come.'

Paul and Michelle followed him to the base of the stairs. It seemed he didn't want anyone to help him with the stairlift now either, so it took longer than necessary for him to get himself seated. They walked up the stairs beside him.

'Someone came to see me yesterday afternoon,' he said.

'In a dark BMW,' Paul stated. He recalled the modern suit on the long, slender body, the curly ponytail and the cocky stride as the guy headed for the front door.

'So you saw him. He's an … an associate.'

'Yes?'

'Or let's call him that. Ernesto Rodrigo.'

'An associate.' The word had the ring of business and respectability, but Paul made it clear he knew better than that.

'We've done plenty of business.' Bernard frowned. 'Private business.'

'Always legal?'

They had reached the top of the stairs and now Paul and Michelle had to wait for Bernard to transfer himself from the lift to the waiting wheelchair.

'Sometimes.' He stopped Michelle when she went to push him and started wheeling himself over to the study. Over his shoulder he said, 'But mostly it was the kind of thing not everyone needs to know about. I thought this was just another of those times.'

Bernard nudged open the door. They followed him in.

Something that had not been visible from the passage was now the first thing Paul noticed. The kudu trophy looking down on the room from the wall. He didn't doubt that Bernard had shot the animal himself, probably on one of those hunting expeditions that cost people as much as a seaside holiday for which the less well-heeled would spend all year saving. A dead antelope became biltong, but a trophy could stand the test of time, and this graceful head, vanquished but nevertheless proud, commanded attention even in a room filled with antiques, a display cupboard, a safe, bookshelves and, of course, the large desk with its attendant chairs. Its two eyes, dead but shiny, took hold of yours and didn't let go.

Eyes that had looked down on the day Bernard's wife came in here and shot herself.

A head that was now turned on the man who had shot it, but who would never again lie in wait for buck in the veld.

Bernard was behind the desk and put his hands on the broad desktop. 'I was sitting *here* and that bastard Rodrigo came in and stood where you're standing now.'

'And?'

'And then he put down in front of me what he had brought along.'

Yes, Paul remembered how the light-grey briefcase had swung from the man's hand as he walked towards the front door.

'What was inside? Money?'

'Money he owed me. He said something like … or no, these were his exact words: "Here is the three point two you've been carrying on about."'

'Three point two million,' echoed Paul.

'Can't be a coincidence. What do you think?'

'No, not a coincidence. And I take it he wasn't exactly eager to hand it over.'

'No. I'm afraid I … well, yes, you know, that I might have been a little sarcastic. I told him it hadn't killed him to bring it over after all. He sat down and glared at me. Then Lindsey stuck her head in and asked if he'd like a drink. He was friendlier then. He did look at her, but I didn't think—'

Paul interrupted, 'Where's the money now?'

Bernard pointed at the upright safe to his left. 'Still just like that, in the briefcase he brought. He said it could stay until I had to hand *him* money in it again. I was thinking that that would be the bloody day.'

Paul looked at the safe. So, not all millionaires had the small type that you saw hidden behind paintings in movies. This one, tall and grey, would have swallowed the briefcase with ease.

'Rodrigo's making it clear to me that it's him.' Bernard's voice was strained. 'And that he wants the money back.'

'I don't know the way you two worked things, but he could simply have refused to hand it over in the first place?'

'God knows what goes on in that mind. Those guys ... talk about lying down with dogs, right? He wants me to know it's him, that's why it's the exact same amount, and I can't do anything about it. I tried calling him this afternoon. The bastard won't answer.'

'If you knew it was him,' Paul asked, 'was that why you knew it couldn't have been a black man calling?'

Bernard raised his shoulders. 'It might have been. It *did* kind of sound like it. But I knew that really it was him, Rodrigo. He could have asked someone to call on his behalf. He has a big ... organisation.'

More like a syndicate, Paul thought.

Bernard opened a drawer and took something out.

Michelle's inhalation hissed in her throat.

'I want you to take this along,' said Bernard. 'When you and Michelle go.'

Paul felt as if his legs were disappearing right beneath him. The black object was being held out to him. It was like a fat snake slithering into a playground, abruptly but undeniably *there*. And all the rules you had set up since leaving the sort of world in which such a thing could happen suddenly no longer counted for anything, because when all was said and done the playground still remained a part of that world.

'Do it now,' orders the man with his arm around Mike's throat, the pistol to his head.

You need to make a decision, you, standing there with a pistol of your own, and you make it, raise the firearm, your finger taut on the trigger.

Then the shot. The way your arm jerks … the way the little dot appears on Mike's forehead.

'I don't believe in that stuff.' It didn't sound like his own voice. He remembered how he had thrown up the one time he tried to force himself to do some target practice.

'But you were a policeman,' Bernard reminded him.

'Not anymore.'

Paul was aware of Michelle beside him. *She* knew. *She* would understand, but not Bernard, and he wasn't going to share the reason with him.

'Here! It's for your protection.'

Bernard was still holding it out to him; the butt was designed for a steady grip. Paul remembered how he had repeatedly come close to dropping it that night. How slippery his palms had been, just like they were now.

'I'm not touching it.' He looked away and met the gaze of the kudu, which stared back coldly.

31

Night fell. A greater silence descended over the valley; more stars appeared to offer light.

Paul tossed and turned. He was sure Bernard and Michelle weren't sleeping either.

He heard an owl. It had to be the one he'd heard on the first night. If only he'd taken it for what it traditionally is: an omen.

Except that owls are everywhere, which means they are harbingers of nothing.

The man – or men – wouldn't call now. Tomorrow, almost certainly tomorrow. It would be more effective to wait longer, but he doubted they'd have that much patience. A few more hours and the owl would be gone, Mary's rooster would be crowing, and what had to happen would happen.

If he could just manage to get some sleep. He knew he wouldn't be afflicted by the same series of images now.

He was in a brand-new nightmare.

DAY 4

32

It seemed this morning might turn out sunny as well, and through the open window came the chirping of birds, indicating that all was well in the avian kingdom. Less so inside the house.

At the dining table, Paul pushed his empty plate aside. Bacon with two fried eggs again, and the fried tomato and a slice of bread. It seemed this was the permanent breakfast offering. Everything in a little lagoon of oil, making him suspect that Johnny was planning to kill them all off through high cholesterol, although this was probably also as Mary had prescribed.

He'd barely tasted the food, but had forced it down since it meant energy. His stomach was in a knot and he was shaky and it wouldn't do to be hungry on top of it all.

He was about to get up when he heard footsteps on the stairs. A few seconds later Michelle walked in.

She gave him a neutral look – which turned to a smile only once she had checked they were alone. She looked tired; she looked the way he felt. Still desperately desirable, though that was the last way Paul would describe himself this morning. She had just sat down opposite him when Johnny peered through the swing door.

'Morning. I'm coming with your food.'

'Thank you, Johnny. Could you please take something up to Bernard? To the study. He's not coming down. I don't know if he'll eat anything, but ...'

The swing door had already closed. Johnny's unpleasant expression had been quick to return. He clearly didn't like orders or even requests from someone who had arrived here with as little money as himself.

Money, thought Paul, it was all about money.

It *had* been a little wilful. Michelle could have taken the food up herself.

'Bernard is waiting for them to call,' she said.

'Hmm.'

Paul remained aware of how much more weight there was to the right side of his jacket than the left – it was his own jacket; no chauffeur's uniform today. Heavier because he had capitulated the night before.

Fuck it, Paul, I'm not telling you to shoot the bastard. Who says I won't take care of that later? But you can't go empty-handed.

He still hadn't wanted to take the firearm the man was holding out to him, but Bernard had insisted.

Take it along in case something happens. In case you need to protect my two girls.

And there is such a thing as fairness. He wanted to take something from Bernard. A 'girl'. If he had so much as a shred of honour, he owed it to the man to bring back the other one. Never mind that he'd had no indication from Michelle that she would indeed consider taking off with him. Never mind that it went against her long-term plans and that it would mean the end of her cosy existence. Yesterday he had felt both their defences going down, but the euphoria of sex could convince you of anything. The same could be said of the afterglow, but now this new thing had come between them.

The pistol was so heavy that he wanted to ditch the jacket, but he had to get used to the weight in the right-hand pocket.

'Did you manage to get some sleep?' he asked.

Michelle raised her eyebrows. 'Does it matter?'

'Of course it matters.'

'Not a wink. You're not the only one scared of guns. I'm terrified of the things.'

For a moment she looked so threatened that he wanted to say something, but he didn't know quite what. He also wanted to reach across the table and take her hand, but just then Mary went past the open door that led to the hallway.

33

Bernard sat at his desk, his breakfast all but untouched. He had tried eating, but felt his stomach start to heave.

He looked down at his cell phone.

Fucking mute piece of technology.

What if he never heard from Ernesto Rodrigo again – or whoever it had been on the phone?

He *would* call again, had to. He was after the money.

But what if it was all about revenge? There were so many people who had good reason. Because of him, his child was …

Don't torture yourself like this!

He turned and looked out the window to see a strip of greenery with deep-purple mountains in the background, and above it all the cerulean sky that he'd never seen elsewhere. It was breathtaking, but it meant nothing without Lindsey here.

Then it rang. The phone was ringing!

Bernard grabbed it, nearly dropped it, jabbed at the answer button.

'Yes.'

34

Michelle gripped the steering wheel as if it were a lifebuoy – which couldn't be more ironic, seeing as she was using it to take them into the danger zone.

They were in her red Citi Golf, which was so far from new it now barely qualified as red. This was what the man had specified when he called Bernard: they had to take her car, and she had to drive. They had already made their way through Riebeek-Kasteel and now they were going up the hill towards Riebeek West.

So quickly! Despite a few hours, Paul didn't feel like he'd had any time to prepare. Where was his strategy? His Plan B? He had to fall in with others' plans and orders, things were moving along, it was a great big river dragging him down with the rest of the flotsam. There was the call, the specifications of how and where, and then it was all under way.

Time flies when you're *not* having fun. Boom-boom went his heart, but he had to appear calm for her sake.

'What are you looking at?' Michelle turned her head towards him, her eyes hidden behind her sunglasses.

'I'm looking at how beautiful you are.'

'God, Paul, not now.'

But she took the sting out of it with a little smile and gave his knee a squeeze.

'You'll find the place easily?'

Her attention was back on the road. 'I've been past there a few times.' She exhaled through her nose. 'Even though I barely noticed it at the time.'

There was something he had wondered about. 'You really didn't consider *not* coming? You could have said no.'

She looked at him again. Her mouth gave nothing away and he wondered whether her eyes, behind the shades, revealed anything more.

'You know how much money is lying here behind us.' At once she sounded less tense, almost playful. 'You realise, of course, if we had the tiniest bit of sense, we'd just keep driving.'

There it was on the back seat: the light-grey briefcase holding more banknotes than he had ever seen, and probably would ever see, all in one place.

'But then neither of us has the least bit of sense.'

He said it just as lightly as she had, but it had startled him, as she had likely intended. That *was* what she wanted; it was a joke, and not a hint, surely?

'And we have to do the right thing.'

He wondered if she was testing him. Wondered if she was waiting for him to make the suggestion now that she had created that chink. If he said let's do it, there was the possibility that she'd react with shock and ask him if he was mad – or she would agree to the plan and keep on driving.

'We have to do the right thing,' he said.

They pressed on, bringing them closer and closer to their destination. These were the quiet moments before … before whatever would happen. The time in which he had to get himself into the right frame of mind. *That* was what he had to keep thinking about.

She gave him a few more seconds of her profile, then looked at him and smiled. 'Relax. I'm pulling your leg.'

'You!'

Who was the great actor now? He'd sounded as if he had believed her.

He remembered the two of them up in his bed. The thought she had expressed and which she clearly had given a lot of thought. *To be able to keep getting away, you need money. Plenty of it.*

Paul looked at his watch. 'It's nearly ten. We mustn't be late.'

Keep your eyes on the goalpost. Don't get paranoid and start imagining all kinds of ridiculous scenarios. He had something important to do, he and this woman together.

But the images streamed into his mind involuntarily, and she was in each of them. Michelle serving Bernard and his wife in the restaurant. Michelle looking somewhat like Mrs Russell. Michelle, as in the dream he'd had, putting a pistol to Mrs Russell's head.

You're letting your mind run away with you, you're not thinking straight. This is the woman you wanted to run away with!

Still want to run away with.

Michelle contacting Ernesto Rodrigo, or him contacting her; or maybe they'd known each other before she had moved down here, and then one of them had come up with this bright idea.

Michelle who, each time it occurred to her that all the luxury surrounding her was merely on loan, consoled herself with the knowledge that it wouldn't be much longer before—

'It's right over there,' she said, jerking him back to reality.

35

They weren't far from the building. Tin roof. It might have been a factory once. Though the walls were still standing, the place was in noticeably bad shape, grass and weeds thriving. There was only one floor, but it was extensive.

Plenty of trees and shrubs. Places to hide.

The main entrance was to the right. Paul could tell from where he was that the door was no longer there, only a large hole.

They were being watched. He could feel it.

It also felt as if someone had a hand on his throat.

They were already about a kilometre from the turn-off and the dirt road was partially overgrown. But there were tyre tracks; another car had been here recently. It might be hidden behind any of a host of taller bushes.

No other buildings nearby. There was fuck all around.

Michelle stopped the Golf a few metres from the building and turned off the ignition.

Each second that passed brought them closer to what would be.

And what was that? His palms were covered with sweat – as they were that night, but he couldn't think about that now. It was morning and he was somewhere completely different. Just go do it, like you would have before. Think like you did in those days. It's just an exchange: you hand something over, you get something in return. Your life's been in danger so many times anyway, and you're still here. Danger is simply a part of who you are. You've walked away from it so often without as much as a scratch.

But he was no longer that fearless guy. He never had been; it was just an illusion that he had believed in and which other people fed. Sandra Menzies and other admirers. And he did so badly want people to think he was the cat's whiskers, until the real test arrived.

Death. That's what Mike got for relying on him.

'Ready?' Michelle took off her sunglasses.

Now she would open her door. There was no stopping it.

Were those honest eyes looking at him? He had to trust her. He had no choice. She was either unbelievably brave being here or she knew she had nothing to fear. Which would mean he did, because he was the only one who could prevent her from taking off with the suitcase.

Stop imagining things!

'Ready.' He got out. Took in the scent of the earth. The dust. Silence so intense they might as well have been on another planet. Of the road Paul could hear nothing, but then he recalled how few cars they had seen.

He pulled out the briefcase. Closing the back door made more noise than he had intended, and he gritted his teeth. But it wouldn't make a difference. It was no secret that they were here.

He held the briefcase out to Michelle.

She hesitated, then took it.

All was as the man had prescribed: *she* had to carry it.

She was about to take a step, but stopped. Paul did the same, and then cursed himself for it. He was meant to be the strong one, he was the man, the ex-cop!

The hairs rose on his neck and his palms were wet. But he had to remember this wasn't about him, it was about Lindsey. Do it for her. That's why you came, and now you're here, so do it.

It was a factory, a deserted place, nothing more. It was just the locale for an exchange. He had to erase the images that kept trying to obscure the present.

And this is the place. You and Mike are almost there. Derelict, unlike the rest of the houses in the street. The nearest streetlamp is dead, but the moonlight reveals rows of broken windows.

Inside Alistair Bogart is hiding out, or quite possibly he is.

Mike trots towards the house without a word, you follow, it happens so quickly, he's already beside the front door.

'I don't know if I'm up for this,' said Mike.

Paul blinked. It didn't sound like Mike.

Of course it wouldn't – it was Michelle talking.

And then they were at the entrance. This wasn't a derelict house, but a derelict factory. There were plenty of differences. They weren't on either side of the entrance but next to each other in front of it, and they would be going in together.

He had to note the differences, not the similarities.

There were mountains behind them and they were in a green valley, not in a suburban street with houses in a mishmash of styles. And it wasn't as quiet as he had imagined: there were birds chirping because it wasn't dark like that other time either; here they were in broad daylight.

'It will be over soon,' he tried to reassure Michelle. Wanted to find strength in the words himself.

But it would have to get worse before it could get better.

Mike. Michelle. Her name pretty much came down to the female form of Mike. Together they had stepped into that place … and look how that had turned out! Was this another premonition? Did it mean something would happen to her as well?

You *will* get yourself together!

'Hold on, I'm here.' He was glad to hear how even his voice was. He did not, in fact, sound like someone about to shit his pants. 'We give him the money, we get Lindsey, we leave.'

Tell yourself you're not scared, and maybe you'll stop being scared.

It was time to go inside.

Your breathing. Get it under control. As quietly as you can, you move to the first open door on the left. He could be waiting for you there.

There are so many places he could be. Another door on the right, and then there's another on either side before the turn in the passage.

You hold the pistol out in front of you, as you were trained.

Ready.

They were already deep into the big, dark space. It was like a hall. When did they get all the way over here?

It was because he was in two places. But it was right here where he damn well had to stay.

In reality it wasn't all that dark; his eyes had adjusted to the light. And while the sun was on the other side of the building, there was enough light coming through the broken windows for him not to trip over anything.

It was nothing like that other place.

Apart from the fact that it felt the same, and then it was one and the same thing.

And, unlike that night, he wasn't holding a pistol either. It was still in his pocket. He was glad it was there.

Take it along in case something happens. In case you need to protect my two girls.

Bernard, it so happens I kill people when I try to protect them this way.

Had it maybe been a tannery, this building? He wasn't sure what made him think that. But when the business had gone under, it had been the beginning of the end for the building that used to house it. Paint peeling from the walls and falling plaster helped to tell the sad tale of the country's economy. Every light in the place had been broken. In any case, the power would have been shut off a long time ago. Not far away, Paul saw a dried-out dusky-brown heap where someone had used the floor as a toilet.

He remained aware of how much heavier his jacket was on *that* side.

Then, a sudden hissing sound behind him – he nearly whipped around but then realised it was Michelle. She had only exhaled a little too loudly.

One thing was sure: Lindsey wasn't out here in the open. It would have been too easy, and nothing is easy. They would have to go further inside.

There were three doors on the left. Or, more to the point, one door half-open, and two rectangular holes where there used to be doors.

'There's no one here,' Michelle whispered. She was right beside him and her fear was plain to see.

'We have the money. He'll be here.'

'We would have heard by now …'

'He's here somewhere.'

Paul walked up to the half-open door and peered inside. It led into another hall, this one smaller than the first. He supposed workers used to clock in here in the morning before heading to machinery that was long gone. Now there was just dust and cracked walls; those windows that were still filled with glass were filthy.

At the other end, another door.

'We're here!' he called out. Michelle jumped with fright. 'We have it on us!'

No answer.

Only echoes.

Here! On us!

Here! On us!

They looked at each other and walked to the next door – or rather, the hole. From the doorway it appeared as if there weren't even any windows in that section. The doorway was a rectangular block of nothingness.

The turn lies ahead and you become even more anxious. For a second you are convinced the passage won't veer to the left as it should. You will take that corner and it will swallow you like a python.

Stop it, fucking stop it!

They headed into the darkness. He led the way. Something was still gripping his throat. When he tried to take a deep breath, he thought the dust would suffocate him.

The guy has no reason to kill us, he tried to reassure himself. We're bringing the money and that's all he's after.

And it wasn't pitch dark ahead and around him, there was some light coming from behind.

But not enough for him to be able to tell whether there was another room after this one. Whether there was an open or a closed door at the other end, or nothing at all.

Instinct told him they had reached a dead end and would have to return to the first room. To the other two options, those doorways. The man was on the other side of one of those two.

Lindsey as well.

What if she wasn't there? The man had simply come to pick up his money. Lindsey was already dead and now it was their turn to die.

Paul turned around and Michelle followed. Out through the closest door, retracing their steps, out through the next door – and each time everything inside him went taut, as he expected to find someone around the next corner.

When they were back in the main hall he shouted, 'Let's get this over with!'

Over with!

Over with!

He waited.

Silence.

Michelle moved the briefcase to her left hand.

Paul inhaled deeply. He would choke on the dust if he had to.

'The money's here! Everything! Let's make our swap!'

Everything! Swap!

Everything! Swap!

He waited …

And heard something else. He wasn't sure what.

Michelle looked at him and he could tell she had heard it too.

Was it a voice? It hadn't sounded like words.

Paul started moving towards the two doorways and beckoned to Michelle to follow. His hearing had always been reliable and he could swear the sound had come from somewhere beyond the one on the left. He stepped inside, aware of Michelle on his heels.

Again, it wasn't a big room. Just a few metres, then another door. It was open.

A corridor, a long corridor with doors on either side. He could make them out, because at the end there was a half-open door. With faint light coming from behind.

Enough light for him to see where he was going.

All the same it was another dark passage, and so he remembered it, felt it again – that place, that evening.

Managed to sweep it out of his mind.

There was the sound again. Clearer.

Someone groaning.

It couldn't be a man; the pitch was wrong.

Paul picked up his pace, even though he realised it could be a trap. It could all be one big trap, but now he had to get it over with. After all the silence, here, eventually, was a sound, a sign of life, and he had to get to Lindsey. So he stepped it up, wanted to run, really.

Down the corridor, past two doorways, or rather openings, because Lindsey wouldn't be there, the groan had been too muffled to have come from so close by.

The muscles in his neck went taut when he realised how easily someone could have sprung out of one of those places to attack him and Michelle. Where has all your training gone, Paul Mullan?

Or maybe he simply knew that something – whatever it was – was waiting at the end of the passage. Maybe enough police instinct had been preserved.

Nevertheless, he stopped to peer inside when they got to the next opening. In there it was dark too, because now they were in the heart of the building. No more windows, just a narrow strip of daylight breaking through a gap in a sheet of corrugated iron.

Enough light to be able to see that no one was here either.

There were two more openings: one on the left and one on the right.

There it was again. A moan.

Definitely from over *there*!

It was no time to be irresponsible, but he rushed over to the end of the corridor anyway. Poked his head around the door.

Another large room. It was on the other side of the factory, and there were windows here. He could see a lot more.

Including her.

He shoved the door wide open.

'Lindsey ...'

She was half-seated, half-lying about five metres from him, her shoulders and head resting against the dirty wall. When she saw him she groaned more loudly. Couldn't say anything because a dirty, off-white cloth had been tied tightly around her mouth. Her hands were tied behind her back, Paul realised, which explained why she was in such an uncomfortable position. Her ankles were tied too. With ordinary rope.

Her eyes were wild. What was she trying to convey – that the man was close by? He swung his head around, even though he was sure there was no one else there, and took a good look.

Nothing.

'Don't worry, we're here.' He tried to sound soothing, and with the 'here' he was by her side. She looked as if she was on the verge of hysteria. Their arrival must have brought the tension to a head.

Behind him Michelle gasped. 'Paul,' she managed.

Only now he realised what it was ... something on Lindsey's stomach, tied to her, over her clothes. It hadn't escaped his notice, but he'd been too busy seeing to other things to look closely.

A grey box, dull metal.

Explosives.

He went cold inside.

He had never been trained for this. Oh yes, the police do give instruction about this kind of thing, but if it's not your field of expertise, then only in passing. And an expert *had* been coming to fill in his division on home-made bombs, but he had never turned up. Traffic jam or something, Paul couldn't remember. All that he could recall was how pleased he was to have the afternoon off. The little that he did know he had gleaned from the Internet, same as any other sod. Why hadn't he done more reading up on the subject? He knew why. Because he hadn't thought it would ever come in useful – he wasn't in the bomb squad, after all – and because back then he had thought that he was already doing more than enough. And this device was the sort he reckoned anyone could have made by looking it up online. The way he looked at it, it was an amateur job. Not that that made it any less deadly.

A bomb is a bomb.

Stay calm.

But it's a fucking bomb!

A green wire and a red wire poked out of the same hole at the side of the box, then disappeared into another one. On the front, a window with a black button above it, which, Paul assumed, had been pressed to start the timer.

The window displayed four red digits.

02:39

He had a mental flash of a photo he had seen of bomb victims. People ripped apart. Of the few that survived, many wished they hadn't.

The last digit changed: 02:38

The destruction of flesh, the tearing apart. Lindsey with her tiny little figure in pastel dresses.

02:37

Fuck it, no wonder the girl was in such a bad way. She couldn't see the digits, but she had to be aware of the fact that there couldn't be much time left, and …

Two and a half minutes *wasn't* much!

Desperately, he tried to work it out. It was thoroughly attached to Lindsey. Too thoroughly to remove in one hundred and fifty seconds – and time was ticking away. The box was around twenty by fifteen centimetres, pretty small, but size was no indication of the effect it would have if …

'Don't worry, I'll have you out of this in a jiffy,' he said in a reassuring tone that he'd dug up from somewhere. How was he going to cut one of those wires? He had no tools and that's what needed to be done, it was logical. But he still didn't know *which* one.

'Mmmm!' Lindsey rolled her eyes left and right, no, to indicate something *behind* her, but he didn't understand. He went to undo the cloth around her mouth, but she jerked her head away, gestured again.

This time he understood.

A pair of yellow-handled scissors, lying on the filthy cement floor. Small, suited for fine needlework, but they would do the job.

Paul was reaching for them when he heard a scraping sound.

A shoe on cement.

He turned towards Michelle – was it her? No, she was right behind him and the sound was ...

Now he knew where. Coming towards the door through which they had entered.

Michelle was between him and it. He was still on his haunches and couldn't see past her, but his ears picked it up again, hard soles hitting cement, louder now, faster.

She hadn't heard, was still watching him, looking at Lindsey.

He grabbed at the pistol in his pocket. There was no other choice. He wanted to take it out, to use it like he had so many times when he was still a cop, but whereas seconds ago time had been running away from him, now everything was happening slowly ... much too slowly.

He had to get to his feet. He couldn't get it out hunched over like this.

He rose and got hold of the cold pistol, despite his clammy fingers, and pulled. But the barrel was hooked on the inside of his pocket. No! He yanked hard and the fabric tore, releasing the gun. It came out ... it was out.

He had to get Michelle out of the way first. Christ, everything needed to happen so quickly but it wasn't!

Wobbling, he tried to raise the weapon.

'Do it now,' orders the man pressing the pistol to Mike's head. And you need to make a decision, and you make it, have to do it quickly, grasp the pistol, raise it so that the barrel points where it should and pull the trigger.

The shot.

He couldn't. He wanted to lift his arm, but the barrel stayed pointing at the floor.

He saw Michelle's enquiring look.

The pistol shook in his hand.

Terror registered on her face when she realised someone was behind her.

At first, Paul thought she was diving towards him, then he realised she'd been pushed.

She stumbled into him and he lost his balance. Reeled. He had to be careful or he'd step on Lindsey. He started to fall … was heading for the wall … had to break his fall, wanted to put out his hand … the hand with the pistol.

He felt it being wrenched from his grip. And then he managed to break his fall after all – but with his forehead, and everything turned to black.

36

In 60 seconds an enormous number of things can happen.

Worldwide about 250 babies are born.

Lightning strikes the earth around 360 times.

There are five earthquakes, 107 deaths, 18 of which are due to famine.

In 60 seconds an enormous number of things can also happen in a valley where visitors often feel that time stands still.

In a double garage converted into a hair salon in Riebeek West, a woman was busy with her iPad, taking in a 350-word article about some new Hollywood divorce scandal.

A block away a girl was writing an email to her new friend: 103 words, the most she had ever typed in that time.

The town's best rugby player did 23 decent sit-ups.

His athlete pal was jogging a little way out of town: covering 411 metres in that time. At the turn-off he saw the old steel factory in the distance with a red Citi Golf parked close by. Strange. When had anyone last gone *there*? But then he lost sight of it and was ready for the next 60 seconds, the next 400-and-something metres.

Two couples were having sex, one of them married, the other in committed relationships, but not with each other. There were six people who had yet to emerge from bed; people were yabbering on WhatsApp, newspapers were being flicked through, people were dunking rusks in coffee, kissing, baking, sewing and welding, a sheep was being shorn, a man was praying, children were crossing the road, an old lady was getting comfortable on the toilet, a maid was using a vacuum cleaner, housewives were tidying closets, teeth were being brushed, the boy with obsessive compulsive disorder was washing and washing and washing his hands, a beggar was opening the bottle of brandy he had just bought with the money he had collected yesterday, a dog was being fed, gardens were being watered and a mirror polished, doormats were being beaten. Everyday things that didn't mean the difference between life and death, because it was only a minute, wasn't it, and what could really change in such a short space of time?

37

The earth swayed back and forth and a voice came from afar, a voice he could nearly peg, but which most likely didn't normally have quite that ring to it, and there was something familiar to the word being repeated.

Auuuu …

A word, or a name.

Paaaauuuu!

His.

'Oh God, Paul!'

Michelle was bent over him, but she hadn't fully taken shape yet. She was shaking him.

'What …?'

'Paul! Wake up!'

The next moment he was alert and Michelle didn't only sound as if she was going out of her mind, she looked it too, the way her face was distorted. Then he recognised the space, knew where he was, what he had come to do. Remembered Lindsey on the filthy floor.

And here she was beside him, hands tied behind her back and her ankles bound. The cloth was no longer covering her mouth, but she seemed too panicked to get a word out.

Behind Michelle was a pair of legs – someone lying on his back.

'I shot him.' Michelle's voice was uneven. 'He …'

Paul remembered the pistol being jerked from his hand. She was clutching it in her left hand.

'Paul, you have to do something!'

The explosive device.

Fear flashed through him like lightning, but so did adrenaline, adrenaline which gave him strength. He swung towards Lindsey and saw the grey box, and the red digits on the display.

00:24

Which ticked down to 00:23.

Bomb. A sudden, violent release of energy. Destructive power.

His mind was as clear as it would ever be. He scooped the yellow scissors from the floor, struggled to get his thumb and index finger through the holes, because they'd been designed for smaller hands. He leaned over Lindsey, saw her terrified brown eyes looking up at him, opened the blades, got them either side of the green wire.

00:17

Ready to cut.

But what if …?

He froze. He could see it so clearly, the explosion that would come from choosing incorrectly. He could swear he felt it already.

If he didn't choose, it would happen in any case. None of them would survive. Shock, heat, fragmentation, shrapnel, broken bones.

Panic. There had been times he'd wished to die, but he'd only just found something to give him hope again. For that he had to stay alive.

00:09

'Paul!' shouted Michelle at his back. 'Dammit, Paul!'

A burning sensation, that's what would precede the great nothingness, then they'd look like the hunks of meat Mary and Johnny work with in the kitchen.

He moved the scissors.

The red wire.

For no other reason than the fact that red would normally not be the one people chose.

He cut.

The wire held, it was strong, it wouldn't let itself be cut.

Fuck!

With as much control as he could muster, he forced his thumb and index finger together …

00:04

Just don't let the scissors break, not now. He felt the wire start to give, but whether it would yield in time, he didn't know. It felt …

00:01

The blades met.

He was waiting for it, the punishment for making the wrong choice. Was it over? Was this what it felt like to be dead, torn apart? Is this how your body reacts to this kind of shock, behaving as if nothing happened?

Slowly he realised that there had been no explosion. And wouldn't be one either.

It was over!

He heard something fall, metal hitting the floor. The pistol. Michelle had her arms around his neck. She nearly dragged him down, but he got up, held her and felt her body shake against his.

'It's okay,' she said, almost immediately, and he knew it was because she had remembered Lindsey – that she was not to see her in another man's arms, or for no longer than circumstances justified. 'I'm just …'

They leaned over Lindsey. Michelle worked at her ankles, and Paul struggled with the rope around her wrists. It was tightly knotted, but his fingers found a weak spot and it started to come undone.

We're all still alive, he thought. The only dead body was that of the stranger behind them.

Not Ernesto Rodrigo. Clearly not Portuguese. He might have been Nigerian, dressed in the camo gear you found in some menswear departments – thick drill, brown and taupe, suited to hiding out. Big build, broad shoulders and a short neck that made his rather small head seem almost directly attached to his chest. His full lips, darker than the rest of his face, were open.

His eyes were also open, his head turned slightly. The bullet had hit him in the forehead and most of the blood had streamed down his cheeks and pooled on the floor forming a dark frame around his head. Some blood had collected in his left eye.

It would have been him talking to Bernard on the phone.

He must have been waiting outside, following them once they'd entered. The idea would have been for him to grab the briefcase from Michelle and run off while they were working on Lindsey. He would have probably adjusted his plans if they hadn't found her quickly enough, and there was only a minute or so to go before the thing exploded. Setting off in the wrong direction first, they almost certainly took longer than he had estimated.

Whatever the case, it hadn't worked out for him.

A few minutes later, Paul Mullan walked out into the sunshine, and never had it felt so good. Michelle carried the briefcase, and he held Lindsey with one arm, the explosive device in his other hand.

'Give it here,' she said suddenly, struggling free and grabbing it before Paul could stop her. Blinded by rage, Lindsey flung it to one side. He only saw the nearby hole when the piece of equipment that had nearly cost them their lives disappeared into it.

Paul wanted to get closer to see how deep the hole was, but then Lindsey was back beside him. She pressed her head to his chest and her shoulders were shaking as she sobbed. He felt her warm breath through his shirt. He held her close.

Over her head, he looked at Michelle. Who was turning away.

The bomb had been deactivated. It couldn't do any harm now.

When Lindsey pulled her head away and wiped her cheeks, probably a full minute later, the three of them walked over to the Citi Golf.

Driving off, the groaning engine and small stones scattered by its tyres were almost certainly the last noises above a certain volume that would be heard here today; behind them silence descended with the settling dust.

38

Early afternoon, and Paul was standing in the sunshine. Every cell in his body was still on high alert.

There was no way to let off steam here. In the police it was standard procedure to get to a drinking hole as soon as possible after an event like the one of this morning. And perhaps, as all those pent-up feelings had to get out, to pick a fight with some outsiders for good measure. He and Mike had got plastered like this a bunch of times, just the two of them, or occasionally in a bigger group, and would go over everything that had happened – what they had thought and what they had done next – again and again. The facts were replayed much like the highlights of a rugby match your team had won. Another victory for Team Life.

Today I did something right again for a change, Mike.

He had hardly been firing on all cylinders, but he'd been where he was supposed to be. No, he hadn't managed to use the pistol – the fact that Michelle had had to do the shooting in the end made him want to blush – but at least he had managed to hold it, *intending* to do something with it.

Now it was safely back in Bernard's desk drawer.

This flux and flow within him. Adrenaline, obviously, but more than that. The way his body reacted to the sensation he had believed he would never again encounter outside of the police, despite the country's dismal crime statistics. What had happened in that factory, it wasn't *exciting*; he'd never describe it that way, it was never exciting being under threat. Yet the feeling he was left with was very akin to the way you felt after great excitation, your body unable to settle down and accept the reality that it's all over.

He noticed a figure out of the corner of his eye.

Oh, hell.

Johnny stopped a metre from him. 'Bernard would like to see us all in the lounge.'

'Right.'

'You should be very pleased with yourself.' Paul was about to reply with a surprised thank you, but then Johnny added, 'The hero.'

Oh, fuck it.

'That's not what it's about. How thick *are* you?'

'Now you're his right hand, aren't you?' Johnny turned away. 'The one he uses to wipe his arse.'

It took a supreme effort to keep his mouth shut and walk after Johnny without grabbing him by his ramrod neck. He wondered when the guy had last been given a proper thrashing.

He followed the stiff neck into the lounge, where Bernard's wheelchair was in its customary spot. He sat like a king before his court, but with a soft expression on his face, one which Paul felt rather suited him.

Michelle and Mary were standing to one side, but Lindsey was close to her father and gave Paul a broad smile.

'I'm very grateful to have you all here.' Bernard's voice sounded as if it might break. 'Especially … my child.'

Lindsey gave him a hug. 'Daddy.'

She was close to tears, but it looked as if she had started processing what she had been through. She had taken a decent bath or shower. Her hair shone and her make-up was light.

She could have been lying in pieces in that place right now, thought Paul. With both him and Michelle alongside her.

Bernard's thoughts were heading in the same direction. 'It could have gone down very differently ... had it not been for you, Paul.'

'We were lucky.'

And how true that was, because he remembered how he'd been about to cut the green wire.

He noticed Johnny wipe the cynical look from his face when he saw Mary frown.

'And you, Michelle,' said Bernard.

Now it was Mary's turn to look cynical. And suspicious. Did she maybe wonder whether Michelle had played a role in the events?

Paul recalled his own suspicions in the car on the way to the factory. But when it had come to the crunch, who had done the shooting? He felt bad for having doubted Michelle, now that it was crystal clear she hadn't had anything to do with the abduction. Would she put herself in a scenario in which she might be blown to smithereens?

Only if the guy had been her accomplice. Only if he had just been playing along up to the point where he would outfox her by grabbing the briefcase ...

Stop it, Paul!

'First of all.' Bernard had regained control of his voice. 'We put this business behind us.'

'I never want to talk about it again,' said Lindsey. 'I just want to forget it.'

Paul needed to remind them. 'A man died.'

Because he knew that in the same way Bernard had initially wanted to keep things quiet, he wouldn't want to report the matter now that it was all over and done with. He was in a quandary over what to do next. And what *he* should do next, as an ex-cop. Things like this ought to be reported. Should he get a SIM card and give the police an anonymous tip about where to find a body and a discarded explosive device? That would be a step in the right direction.

But looking at the relief on these people's faces, he wondered if it was really any of his business.

'That man isn't bothering anyone anymore,' Bernard declared. 'He was prepared to blast my child to kingdom come, just to distract you as he snatched the money. What kind of human being is that? If you hadn't known which wire ...'

'I ...'

Paul found that he didn't want to acknowledge under Johnny's gaze that it had been anything other than a smart decision.

'Lindsey only saw one man.' Bernard looked up at her for confirmation, even though they had clearly discussed it. 'The one who took her, the one who's dead now. So we believe it was just him.'

She nodded.

Paul started, 'And ...'

He wanted to ask *What about Ernesto Rodrigo?*

Bernard's eyes indicated *Let it go*. He continued, 'Lindsey threw the thing away in any case. And it doesn't sound as if it was so sophisticated. So, I say we forget about it. Let someone stumble across that bastard's body by accident.'

Paul wanted to object, to say it couldn't work that way. But the dead guy hadn't been playing by the rules. What rules could there be now? Lindsey was back, and the money too, and that was all that counted.

He realised Bernard was looking at him. He waited.

'What the hell, then.'

Bernard smiled. 'So, on to more pleasant matters. I have my child back. Everything is back to the way it was.'

You hope, thought Paul. No one forgets that easily.

Or maybe you do. It depends on who you are. If someone could get over a thing like his wife's suicide so easily – and it seemed Bernard Russell *had* – then this crisis really had ended for him the moment Michelle called him on the drive back to let him know they had Lindsey, and that she was unharmed.

All that would remain undone, in his view, was making Rodrigo pay. If a plan to that effect was being concocted or had even already been set in motion, Paul didn't want to know about it.

'And I have another special person by my side.' Bernard held out his hand and Michelle placed hers in it. 'You stood by us when you could have said no. Or could have taken to the hills.'

You know how much money is lying here behind us. You realise, of course, if we had the tiniest bit of sense, we'd just keep driving.

'Thank you.' Lindsey took Michelle's other hand. 'Thank you. I can't tell you ...'

'It's ...'

Michelle started crying. She didn't make a scene, simply wiped away the tears in her eyes. But more followed.

'I shot someone dead. I can't believe—'

Bernard interrupted her, 'Would you do me the honour of becoming my wife?'

'What?' Her hand stopped on her cheek. She looked astonished. 'I ...'

'I'm asking: will you marry me?'

Lindsey was the one to react. 'Daddy!' She gestured at the other woman. 'Michelle, say yes.'

'I ...' For a split second she caught Paul's eye, then she answered. 'Yes.'

She laughed, then leaned over and embraced Bernard.

Paul managed to unpack a smile, but wondered how convincing it was. There had been way too many emotions in one day.

Even Johnny was showing a few teeth. 'Uh, we need to celebrate.'

'Let's get some champagne,' said Mary, the only one not looking happy or making much of an effort to look that way. 'I'll show you where it is.'

'I know where it is,' Johnny said, but followed nonetheless.

'*Congratulations*, you two!' Lindsey dished out hugs to her father and to Michelle. 'I feel ...' She started talking in more hushed tones and looked towards the door, but Johnny and Mary had already left. 'I can't even say how I feel! We have to go out tonight. Us four, only us. Nothing fancy. Just being together.'

'But we can all be together *here*,' Bernard protested.

Paul wanted to object too. Going out for a celebration – did he need that on top of everything else? His face was hurting from the sustained smiling as he felt one blow after the other raining down on him. He had tried to believe, before, that everything happens the way it is supposed to; now he knew it was bullshit. Things happen, end of. All the roads of the last several months had not led him here to meet his soulmate. Neither mercy nor salvation was waiting for him in the form of love at Journey's End. After her term of duty with a rich, older man, Michelle had not woken up to the idea that true love with someone as poor as a church mouse would indeed be preferable.

You seem very judgemental. Someone like me has a short shelf life.

When he looked into her eyes, he saw nothing but joy there at the idea of becoming Mrs Bernard Russell. He had to beat it as soon as possible. He wasn't going to play chauffeur for the man that had bought her. Bernard would want to get married as soon as possible. Paul would have liked to have left tomorrow, but the reason for doing so might be too obvious; he would have to grit his teeth for a day or two, and then ...

Actually, no, that wouldn't be necessary. Who cared what they thought? If they could work out why he had left, so what? He would be gone.

Lindsey was arguing with her father, he realised. Laughing, lightly, but more firmly than he had seen her talk to him before.

'Daddy, no, we *have* to go out after an announcement like this. I insist. The four of us. And it's my treat.'

39

'You've become really nosy,' he heard Sandra's teasing tone over the line. 'I'm going to start thinking it's you every time my phone rings!'

He'd found he couldn't quite let go. The policeman in him had re-emerged and even though he was still determined to leave as soon as possible, he hadn't yet, and there were still unanswered questions.

So he had walked a little way from the house again and called.

'Uh-huh.'

'Sounds to me you're ready to start working again.'

Jesus, Sandra, he thought, no wonder it never lasted long between the two of us. Besides the fact that you appear to have forgotten what I did to you, it sounds as if you think it might be possible for me to return to a job for which I'm the worst possible candidate, just like I was for you.

She hesitated. Must have found something out. 'Umm, Ernesto Rodrigo, you said?'

'If you'd be so kind. And you promise it's just between the two of us?'

'Paul.' She sounded hurt. He heard the clicking of the keyboard. 'What are you after, the good news or the bad?'

'Always the good *and* the bad.'

'There's a lot about him. Not exactly a choirboy. But that doesn't matter anymore.'

'Meaning?'

'Your friend Ernesto Rodrigo is dead.'

'Oh.' But he concealed his surprise. 'Recently?'

'Very recently,' she told him. 'As in yesterday.'

Yesterday, thought Paul. As in the day before the three point two million was meant to have been handed over to Ernesto Rodrigo or someone representing him. He'd considered the possibility that Bernard might see to something happening to Rodrigo, but yesterday already? No.

Sandra added, 'Shot by his girlfriend.'

'Ah.'

'It's an open-and-shut case. Evidently he beat her up regularly. Yesterday he gave her one punch too many and she shot him. Two witnesses ... You still there?'

'Still here.' Then he looked over his shoulder and saw Lindsey approaching rapidly. 'I have to go. Thank you! Bye.'

He ended the call before Sandra could reply. Thought of how he had just abused her again. He would have to send an SMS shortly to thank her properly. It was just that seeing Lindsey had startled him, her looking so cheerful when he didn't want to let sleeping dogs lie.

Dead dogs.

'Hope I didn't interrupt you.' She looked up at him, her head tilted in that characteristic way. He had missed it. Why couldn't he just transfer his feelings for Michelle to her?

'It's nothing.'

'Doesn't look like nothing.'

'Why, do I look worried?' Paul put on his most indifferent expression.

'I just came to tell you my father isn't feeling well.' Her concern was plain to see. 'Must be the tension. Yes, well, of course it's that. He's got another migraine.'

'Oh.'

'So I feel I can't go out tonight. I have to stay with him. But you and Michelle must.'

'But we can't. Not if he—'

'Of course you can!' she cried out. 'I've reserved a table and everything. It's for seven thirty, and I've already given Mary the evening off, and Johnny's going out, so ...'

'I thought I'd have an early night.'

'But we were going to go out in any case.'

'I thought I'd turn in early before there was even talk of going out. And now that we aren't going anymore ...'

Whether with others around, or the two of them alone, it would be torture sitting in a restaurant with Michelle hours after she had accepted another man's marriage proposal.

Lindsey wouldn't hear of it. 'You and Michelle deserve an evening ... you know, away from it all. Let me do that for you.'

Much as Paul wanted to decline, by this stage even Houdini would have realised that there was no wriggling out of it.

'Will you be okay?'

'Of course!' She laughed. 'Oh, my saviour, I'm glad you're worried about me, but I'm back here now. It's over. That Rodrigo guy wouldn't dare try something like that again. So it's a yes, then?'

40

The sun had disappeared behind the mountains, and all over town windows had been closed, curtains drawn tight and lights turned on.

So too at Journey's End, although Paul had ensured that the doors and windows were closed and locked up long before sundown. No need to be paranoid, but no need to invite trouble either.

But this *was* paranoia. As Lindsey had said, and he had told himself too, it was over. This uneasy feeling was an after-effect, that was all. He was experiencing it more strongly than the rest of them because that's what he was like. Plain and simple.

41

Michelle went down the stairs. She could never walk down without thinking about what had happened to Bernard there.

She could imagine the look of shock on his face as he'd tripped, and how he'd started to tumble down. He must have had his first landing somewhere around here, there must have been a loud noise, somewhat muted by the carpet, and he must have cried out or groaned …

In the lounge she headed for the liquor cabinet, but saw Lindsey was already standing there. She looked as if she had been waiting for her; she must have heard her come down.

'You look beautiful! That dress!'

Michelle looked down. It was deep purple with a shimmer subtle enough for daytime.

'Oh, it's …'

She couldn't say it was just a dress – Bernard had bought it and it might sound like she was criticising his taste. Or Lindsey's. And it was beautiful. It covered up what needed covering, but made all sorts of promises. Before this evening, she had felt self-conscious in front of Lindsey when wearing expensive clothes, because she could imagine the thoughts going through her head, but tonight she felt nothing but good vibes.

'Mary's nightcap.' Lindsey held out a glass, half-filled with brandy. 'I thought I'd pour a big one for her.'

'You sure about this?'

For a moment it seemed Lindsey thought she was talking about the drink, then she smiled. 'Absolutely. Go enjoy the evening. Daddy and I could do with some alone time. And then you and Paul will get the chance to talk for a change.'

Michelle's heart leapt. 'We don't have much—'

'Get to know him. He's really not a bad guy.'

'I didn't think he was.'

Michelle realised she might have created that impression. Had tried so hard not to appear interested that she came across as condescending.

'I hope he'll be here for a long time,' said Lindsey, with the kind of transparency she wished she still had. She had conditioned herself for so long to not give anything away – because then people just kept taking – that she had wondered from time to time how much she was still able to show.

Lindsey began to walk out, but stopped. 'Would you do me a favour? I want to help that father of mine out of bed. He *will* get up and he *will* come have a good time down here with me.' She held out the glass. 'Would you take this to Mary, please? Before she has to come fetch it.'

'Of course.'

Michelle felt strange walking to Mary's room. She had often walked by her door, but it was always shut. She had never been inside.

Even stranger to knock.

The door opened. Mary looked suspicious for a moment, which didn't surprise her, seeing as they were never exactly going to be close friends. Then the woman saw the glass, nodded and raised the corners of her mouth just a little – probably as she reminded herself that this woman, whom she had always viewed as an intruder, was about to become a permanent feature with an enhanced status. She took the glass and shut the door as quickly as she had opened it.

42

The overture to Mascagni's *Cavalleria Rusticana* floated from the speakers. A beautiful composition – one of Bernard's favourites. The intermezzo was lovely too, but he could never quite get into the rest of the opera. It was ironic, actually, that in a work that had been composed mainly for displaying the glory of the human voice, most people preferred the instrumental bits.

Ten past eight, said the grandfather clock.

He was relaxed and his migraine was just about gone. In the hearth, the fire was flickering cheerfully, the flames casting a play of light and shadow on the ceiling.

Lindsey sat on the carpet with her shoulder resting against his right leg. From above he gently stroked her soft hair.

What would he have done if she had been gone forever?

43

It was the same table the three of them had sat at previously, but this time he and Michelle were opposite instead of beside each other, it was dinner not lunch, and all the windows had been closed to keep out the biting chill.

They both had a glass of red wine. Paul had *not* ordered the same kind Bernard always drank.

And it was a different waiter from the time before, when he had touched her leg …

The waiter delivered their starters: springbok carpaccio for him and a spinach and feta phyllo pastry for her.

'So, what's bothering you?' she asked, taking the first bite.

'Me?'

She swallowed. 'Yes, you.'

'Who said something's bothering me?'

'I am. It's no use trying to hide it. Spit it out.'

Since they left the farm half an hour ago, he'd been concentrating so hard on looking comfortable that he'd ended up terribly uncomfortable. He wasn't in the mood for talking either – rather, he wanted to talk, but dared not, because then he'd only voice things that should be left unsaid.

He had bared his soul to her, but she was choosing money. He had been unrealistic and she was a realist. That was all.

'I thought the idea was for us to get out, away from it all.'

Michelle traced her finger around the rim of the glass. 'I think Lindsey meant for us to talk. That's why she insisted we come.'

'Do you think she noticed anything?'

'Us women are sharper than you men.'

Paul felt the space between his eyebrows narrow. Maybe he'd feel better if he could articulate other thoughts. 'Two things are worrying me. First, it wasn't Ernesto Rodrigo you shot this morning.'

Michelle pressed her lips together at this. Then her mouth relaxed, but he'd seen what effect the morning's events still had on her. You don't shoot someone and just get on with your life. Her reaction made him feel again that there was a bond between them, but that was crap, they couldn't be further apart.

Her hand was on the table, though, close enough for him to be able to put his out and … and he wouldn't.

'We know that,' she answered. 'It was one of his cronies.'

'I'm not so sure. Rodrigo is dead. I spoke to an ex-colleague of mine this afternoon. She looked it up. His girlfriend shot him. *Before* what went down this morning.'

'His girlfriend?' Michelle pushed her plate away. She was thinking. 'Maybe he set everything in motion, with an accomplice. And when he died, his accomplice went ahead anyway.'

'Maybe.'

He wasn't sure why he wanted to sweep this idea aside. That was the conclusion he had come to as well.

'It's possible, Paul.' Whispering, she added, 'Now relax. I'm the one who shot a person today.'

He looked at her. What to say to that?

'But we've lived to tell the tale.' She smiled. 'Let it go. You're not responsible for everyone. Everything's all locked up at home, and could you imagine a better protector than Mary?'

44

Every door and window at Journey's End was indeed shut tight. The white plaster walls stood proud; they were built of solid stone. This was no storybook structure of straw or sticks that could be blown down.

Twenty to nine, according to the grandfather clock in the lounge, where Bernard remained with Lindsey sitting on the carpet next to him. Music was still playing softly, a work of which Bernard didn't know the name. He was drowsy and had nearly nodded off a couple of times.

Though the fire had gone down, it was still radiating heat.

But not everything was in sync with the reassurances Michelle had given Paul. Mary, still fully clothed, lay outstretched on her bed. Her room was impeccable, the furniture arranged at right angles. The only sign of anything approaching untidiness was the empty glass on the bedside table. Or no, there was something else – of the four pairs of shoes Mary wore, and which usually had their heels lined up against the wall at this time of night, one pair was still on her feet.

Her mouth was open and she was making sounds that qualified as some kind of light gurgling rather than snoring.

The protector was slumbering.

45

Their main courses arrived: steak for him and grilled salmon for her. Paul's meat was well done, yet tender and flavoursome.

He looked at the beautiful woman opposite him. It wasn't so long ago that she, like the waitress at the counter, had been waiting tables here for a pittance, flashing smiles to try to extricate bigger tips from sometimes demanding clients.

Her relationship with Bernard was a case of working for tips too, he thought wryly. And everything came to a head this morning when she almost lost her life. All the same, the outcome was rosy in terms of finances and now she'd legitimately be the lady of the house.

Jackpot.

No matter how hard he tried, he couldn't remain angry with her. At thirty-four, even he, a man, couldn't disregard the ticking clock; how much more would she be aware of the ravages of time, seeing that the looks of a woman in her position were one of her greatest assets? The more time went by, the less bargaining power you had.

If he had been a rich, older man, what type of woman would he have chosen? The younger, the better, he supposed. Great way to up your status.

Michelle took a sip of her wine then looked at him.

'And the second thing?'

Paul raised his eyebrows. 'What do you mean?'

'You said there were two things worrying you. One, Ernesto Rodrigo wasn't the one who died this morning. And then you were so intent on finishing your carpaccio that you never got round to the second thing.'

In fact, he had decided to let it go. But maybe it would be for the best to get it out in the open.

His eyes met hers. 'Me and you.'

'I wondered when you'd mention that.'

'I didn't know if I should.' He took a large sip of wine and realised he was hiding behind his glass, in case he showed something he didn't want to.

'I told you, you men aren't too sharp. Of course you should.'

He put down the glass. 'You said yes when he proposed.' His tone of voice expressed everything: resentment, frustration, rage, sadness.

'What else could I have said?' Michelle looked almost angry.

He stared at her. 'Does that mean ...?'

'You know how I feel. No man could be *that* stupid.'

'I also know how you feel about money.'

'Do you now?' But her gaze softened. 'If I'd had to choose yesterday, I might have done the wrong thing. Like so many times before! But that was then. This morning you and I went into that place together. I have blood on my hands, life is short, and—'

'Are you serious?'

'Oh, I did get in a panic when I thought of all I'd have to leave behind. I've worked my arse off for it! Always looking good, being pleasant, doing the right thing.' She shrugged. 'But then choosing between him and you turned out not to be so difficult.'

He stared at her and allowed that feeling, the amazing feeling he'd been experiencing but that had been cut off so abruptly this afternoon, to flood through him again.

He couldn't be mistaken. In the end she'd chosen *him*. Without money.

She'll live to regret this, he thought immediately. She'll miss the comfort. The luxury. Disillusionment will soon set in.

But they'd be together. He saw the way she looked at him. It couldn't be true, yet it was.

'We need to talk everything through tonight,' he heard himself say. 'We can't stay in that house if ...'

'I've told you. I know what I want. I want to be with you. It's simple.'

Not enigmatic at all, once you've seen behind the mask, he realised. The truth was she was a lot franker than most people.

'You're dead, dead sure about this?' the doubting Thomas in him asked, even though he didn't really want to give her an opportunity to reconsider. However, if there were bad tidings in store, he needed an indication now. If she had *any* doubts. 'I'm used to life on the move. You aren't.'

She laughed. 'There, you almost made me change my mind!' She became serious again. 'Paul ... it scares me, to be honest. I had everything so nicely worked out. But yes, I'm one hundred per cent certain. And before Bernard I was also used to being on the move. There's nothing you can tell me about it that I don't already know. Now I want to do it with you.'

His smile was so wide, he thought his face was going to split in two.

He remembered the times he had considered ending his own life. He could see himself on that one particular bridge, just as the sun was rising, casting golden rays across the sky. Jumping had felt like the only possible solution, for while he could witness all that beauty around him, he believed none of it would ever resound inside, just as he knew something else would always remain an abstract concept for him. Salvation.

Stepping back had been the right thing to do, for here it was, in the form of this woman.

He grabbed the passing waiter by the sleeve. 'Could we have a bottle of champagne, please? We've something to celebrate!'

46

He was in a faraway place; he wasn't yet certain where. He knew he had been here before, he recognised his surroundings. The brown dachshund staring at him with her face that always seemed to be grinning. The rough grass over which he was running barefoot. The wooden fence that separated this place from the one next door …

He recognised the roof. He was at home, his parental home. They had one of the few thatched roofs in town.

'Bernie!'

His mother was calling him. It meant he was done playing for now. She would have cooked something he liked … roast chicken, it smelt like chicken. Times like these around the table were fantastic. There might be pudding, too.

At times like these, it almost didn't matter that his father shouted at them at night, when he'd been drinking.

But he couldn't go inside. Couldn't move.

'Bernie!'

He couldn't get to his mother, because … What was wrong with his legs? He was about to fall over and there was nothing to hold onto.

His body jerked.

Then he was awake.

He looked down and saw the trouser material covering his withered legs, then saw the little boy again, running over rough grass.

He reached out for her, but Lindsey had left. He couldn't hear her either. She must have gone upstairs.

The log fire was now ashes and only a faint smell of pine remained.

Then he froze.

A scream. Female. His daughter.

The sound cut through the house. Came from upstairs.

'Lindsey!' He wanted to leap up to find out what it was, but of course he was in his wheelchair, the goddamn wheelchair.

Another scream. Even louder. She sounded terrified.

The panic felt like a grenade had gone off inside him. Bernard swung the wheelchair towards the door, forced the wheels to go faster, steered towards the base of the stairs.

'Lindsey!' he called.

Silence.

He pulled himself out of the wheelchair, nearly fell, but started to hoist himself onto the stairlift.

'Mary!' Could she be sleeping *that* soundly? 'Mary!'

He couldn't wait for her to respond. The pistol in the drawer in his study – he had to get to it before he got to Lindsey. The screams had been so loud, her bedroom door had to be open, if that was where she was.

He struggled to think clearly. Had something merely given her a fright? An insect maybe, a spider? Please let it be something like that!

The wheelchair tipped, he hadn't noticed his left leg was pushing against it. It fell over, onto the carpet, but still made a hell of a racket.

Then he was pushing the button to go up, before he was even properly seated.

The stairlift whirred into motion.

Bloody slowly!

'Lindsey?'

A quarter of the way there. Nothing.

Or?

A stifled moan.

Bernard angled his body so he had a better view, but he could see no one at the top of the stairs. He couldn't see Lindsey's bedroom door from here, if it was open …

The chair vibrated beneath him.

Evenly, in no hurry.

47

The waiter set down a small wooden box with the bill inside on the table and moved away discreetly. Paul, who had already said it would be cash, felt for his wallet in his jacket.

'You sure?' asked Michelle. 'I have the money Lindsey offered. She did mean it to be her treat, you know.'

He laughed. 'Tonight is the night that is going to change my – our – whole life. Of course I'm paying.'

'Fine, then!' She laughed too. 'But take your time. I'm in no rush.'

He thought of the house and all its watching eyes. It wasn't that late, Bernard and Lindsey might still be up, and Johnny might already be back, which would mean they'd have to walk in there like two people who'd simply gone out for dinner as planned. Without being the least bit in love.

While he wanted to jump for joy and shout it from the rooftops.

He took her hand and gave it a squeeze. Soon he'd be able to hold it whenever he wanted.

'I'm in no rush either.'

'I'll see if Bernard is still up when we get back.' Michelle hesitated. 'Or maybe I'll wait till tomorrow to tell him.'

If Bernard were still none the wiser by lights out, she'd have to share his bed. Naturally, this was not what Paul had in mind.

'It won't be easy,' she sighed.

Paul handed the box back to the waiter and lifted his hand to indicate that no change would be necessary.

And they left.

This time it was Michelle at the wheel. It didn't feel to him as if they were the same people who set off for that other place just this morning.

In this car they would leave Journey's End. When? Tomorrow? Yes, tomorrow. They'd have to get out of there as soon as everyone was aware of their betrayal.

'Haven't changed your mind?'

'About wanting you?' She took the turn-off onto the dirt road.

'Yes.'

'No, Mr Mullan. I want you.'

'Oh, you *want* me?'

Her voice became throaty. 'I want you in my life! I want you in my heart!' Then, suggestively, 'I want you in my bed ... but God only knows where we might be sleeping tomorrow night.'

Did that matter? He'd sleep in this car if he had to, as long as she was by his side. Or on the ground. Cold, wet ground!

He remembered them clinking glasses in the restaurant. 'To you,' he'd said.

'No, to you.'

'To us.'

'To us.'

He had yearned for such moments with her. Now he could have a lifetime of them.

They both went quiet as the house came into view. Paul noticed there was no light coming from *that* room on the top floor. Was Bernard up or was he asleep?

They didn't say a word as Michelle parked in the smaller of the two garages. The spot next to hers was empty, which meant Johnny wasn't in yet. They didn't speak as they got out either.

Paul wanted to pull her close but didn't do it.

They walked over to the front door. Shoes on gravel. Other than that, just the sounds of the night.

She unlocked the front door and they entered the house quietly. Like criminals.

All was quiet. There was a light on in the lounge, but no one called out a hello.

Then Paul saw the wheelchair parked neatly at the foot of the stairs – conclusive proof that Bernard had already gone upstairs.

He wanted to touch Michelle, but she gestured that he shouldn't. He understood. It was different in the restaurant, which didn't belong to Bernard Russell.

'Glad they left the lights on.' He wanted to take her hand anyway, needed to, precisely because it was Bernard's house.

Didn't get that far.

'Of course the lights are on. I'm still up.' Lindsey had appeared in the door to the lounge so quickly it startled both of them.

'Lindsey!' said Michelle. 'Oh, so you haven't—'

'Paul.' The girl smiled. 'Surely you'll have a little drink with me first.'

He didn't want to stare, but couldn't help noticing that her dressing gown wasn't quite done up. Though it had pockets and was on the baggy side, it was nevertheless revealing in that it offered a hint of breast. It was the first time he had seen Lindsey look remotely sensual.

He tried to get away. 'I'm afraid I've had more than enough to drink, I think I should go—'

'Oh no, I insist. A drink with my saviour. Please? Besides, I need to chat to you about something.'

He hesitated. Odd moment. He wondered whether she had noticed something between him and Michelle. Could be, because she hadn't invited Michelle to stay. And she had already thanked him.

'Okay.'

Lindsey smiled. 'Goodnight, Michelle. You'd best go up quietly. And don't turn on the light. Daddy's migraine came back.'

Michelle nodded. 'Night, you two.' She had no choice but to leave.

Paul followed Lindsey into the lounge. She walked over to the liquor cabinet, poured, and returned to where he was standing with a glass of brandy in each hand.

He sipped at the amber liquid, pretending not to notice she stood in such a way that her dressing gown was now gaping wider at the top.

48

Gingerly, Michelle pushed the door open.

She was still in two minds – but no, if Bernard was awake, she had to tell him now. Each moment she didn't speak up, she was being unkind. It wasn't fair to keep him in the dark.

Dark also described their bedroom. Only a sliver of moonlight came in through the curtains.

Bernard lay on his side of the bed with his back to her. The wheelchair was a little way off, where she usually parked it after helping him into bed.

It looked as if … yes, the covers were pulled way up, nearly over his head.

'Bernard?'

He didn't answer. Even if he wasn't asleep, his bearing in no way invited conversation. Michelle couldn't deny the feeling of cowardly relief as she shut the door softly. *Really* softly, now that she had been given a reprieve.

She was so excited about all the long-neglected, essential emotional things her future suddenly held again that tiptoeing back was difficult. She wanted to dance!

Her mind replayed scenes from the restaurant as she moved to the chair on her side of the bed. Then she switched on the light in the en-suite bathroom and opened the door a crack.

Just enough light to prevent her from tripping over something.

Quietly she rid herself of her clothes, letting them fall onto the chair. She slipped her white nightgown, which was always draped over the back, over her head. She didn't want to hang up her dress, because that would mean walking down Bernard's side of the bed. And the wardrobe door always creaked.

Every night she'd come up to this room with him. The price she'd had to pay. Odd to think it was over.

He had been good to her sometimes. Quite often. He could make her laugh, actually, when he was relaxed.

She remembered the day she met him; she'd been reminded of it again when she and Paul were sitting in the restaurant. Bernard had waited for his wife to go to the bathroom before calling her over. Pointing at the open wine bottle, he asked, 'Given that this is a screw-top, why do you charge a corkage fee?'

She knew he was looking for the slightest reason to talk; his interest was plain.

'Because otherwise we'd have to charge a screwage fee.'

He was still laughing when his wife got back. Michelle could feel him looking at her occasionally and knew it was just a matter of time before he got hold of her phone number and called.

His personality was still strong – overly so – but so little remained of the robust man she had met that day she couldn't help but feel sorry for him, which he would have found deeply insulting.

She looked in his direction again. He was very quiet. Wasn't snoring, but that might have been because he was lying on his side for a change.

Was he awake after all?

Michelle went into the bathroom and was on the point of closing the door behind her when she stopped.

This was decidedly odd. Her bottles and tubes were displayed on the marble counter as usual, but nearly half of them were missing. As were her toothbrush and toothpaste. Bernard's handful of toiletries were all in place on the other side of the basin.

Why would he have wanted to move them? Or throw them out? Had he maybe knocked them off and broken them by mistake? But the toothbrush and toothpaste?

Mary perhaps? But why?

She really didn't want to go to bed without brushing her teeth, so she poked her head around the door.

'Bernard?' She spoke softly, not wishing to startle him. 'Some of my toiletries seem to have vanished. Do you know anything?'

He didn't stir.

Michelle pulled her head back and closed the door. She'd wash her face at least and dab on some night cream. As her mother had taught her. Back when her mother was still speaking to her.

Should the day come when your stepfather suddenly makes it clear that he is more interested in you than in your mother, it certainly puts love to the test. Her mother had felt threatened – that's the explanation she came up with later, when she was older and had better insight into the workings of the human mind. As a teenager she simply knew her mother wouldn't believe her when she said the creature had started pawing her. Her mother was furious, saying she had made up the story for attention.

That was the first time she had run away.

Now your years of drifting are over, she reminded herself.

She opened the tap and splashed her face.

49

Even with the door closed, Bernard was motionless, sweating. How long had he been lying like this? He couldn't be sure, but the fear remained constant, searing.

It had become even worse when Michelle had entered the room. He was certain she'd be shot.

But then she got undressed, went to the bathroom …

He couldn't answer when she spoke to him. His orders.

In the faint moonlight he could only just make out the black glove, right in front of him.

The hard, cold barrel of the revolver was pressed against his forehead.

50

'Things have changed since you got here, Paul. It feels as if I've known you for years. Or maybe I just don't know enough men!'

Lindsey's head was again tilted slightly as she looked up at him, but the habit didn't make her seem as timid as it had some other times. Maybe it was the shock of what had happened. Sudden trauma did cause unusual changes in behaviour. They should have taken her to a doctor immediately.

It wasn't high-wattage seductive behaviour, but there was an element of coquetry. Or perhaps he was imagining things because he had something to hide.

He remained standing. Had stifled one pretend-yawn so far. Lindsey didn't take a seat either, but took a sip of brandy.

'Well, the guys around here, that's their loss,' said Paul.

She laughed. 'That ... is the correct answer. But maybe the guys around here aren't who I have in mind.'

That look again, summing him up. And he knew she was interested. But she shouldn't have chosen tonight of all nights to tell him this. Tomorrow she'd know how things stood, after Michelle had spoken to Bernard.

He had to get to his room. Immediately. He put down his almost untouched glass. 'Sorry, Lindsey, I'm toast. Time for me to—'

'I'm not going to beat around the bush any longer. You know what I'm thinking.'

'Maybe we shouldn't—'

'I know I'm not your first choice.' She sounded almost impatient. 'I'm not blind. I wanted the two of you to get it out in the open tonight. And my guess is you did.'

'Well ...'

Accusingly now: 'You've only had eyes for her since you got here.'

'If you knew that, why—'

'Maybe I have a head for business, like my father.' At once she sounded like a high-powered executive. 'Or maybe I'm realistic. You can't expect to have everything. But enough – you can ensure that you get enough.'

'Lindsey, what are you trying to say?'

'In this life you have to look out for number one. And you, Paul, need to look out for *yourself*. You've made your choice, but maybe you haven't quite given it enough thought.'

He was about to tell her that he was done thinking, but she raised her hand with such force that half her brandy splashed from the glass.

'Let me be straight, Paul. I'm going to inherit a lot of money. And perhaps sooner than you might think.'

51

Bernard could hear Michelle in the bathroom, even with the door closed.

She had an evening ritual. In the mornings, too, but more so before bedtime. Cream to remove her make-up, something for deep cleansing, something to shrink her pores …

What would happen when she was finished? Why hadn't Johnny done anything yet? The dirty bastard was still lying here beside him, holding the gun against his forehead; keeping it in place.

He was still in the grasp of shock – it was as if more was paralysed than his legs.

What was happening here *couldn't* be true.

Never before had the stairlift seemed so slow-moving. And after that he had to get himself into the upstairs wheelchair.

No more screams, no more moans.

The study door wasn't quite closed. He went closer. Pushed it open.

Lindsey and Johnny were standing there, Johnny with a pistol in his gloved hand. *His* pistol?

No, it was a revolver.

In the blink of an eye Bernard absorbed it all, especially the way Lindsey was looking at him.

Mockingly.

'Daddy, I wish you could see your own face.'

'But ...' What about the screams? He couldn't get his brain to work.

'What did you think was happening?' Still mocking. And now businesslike. 'Actually nothing has happened yet. But it's *going* to. We just have to get something we need from here first.'

The revolver in Johnny's hand was pointed at him, not at her. Even though it was crystal clear, Bernard still had a hard time coming to the only possible conclusion: that she and Johnny had sat down together to craft a plan against him.

'What—'

'Keep quiet. I'll talk when there's talking to be done.'

'Lindsey ...'

Then she hit him.

His ears rang. His cheek was numb where it had been struck. His soft Lindsey hitting him like that?

'Shut up, I said.' She pointed at the safe. 'You need to get it out for us.'

He knew what.

As he removed the briefcase, he heard rather than saw her open the desk drawer and take out the pistol.

And now Johnny was slowly getting up next to the bed. He had finally removed the revolver from Bernard's temple, but kept it pointed at him as he carefully retreated to the bedroom door. He opened it softly. Halfway.

He returned, careful not to kick over the briefcase where he had left it on the floor – something else Michelle had not noticed in the dark.

Johnny took up a position at the foot of the bed, his head turned slightly towards the half-open door, his bearing that of someone who was listening intently.

52

'It's not a bad offer I'm making,' the young woman said to him in this strange new voice.

'Lindsey, that's not the way love works.'

Paul wanted to believe that he knew now how love was meant to work. Before Michelle, he'd been pretty clueless. He wanted to go to bed, hopefully not have any nightmares and wake up tomorrow morning with the knowledge that it was the day he and she would leave. How and if Lindsey got her act together wasn't his concern.

'That's exactly how it works,' she said with conviction. 'You take what you want. Or you buy it.'

He tried a little humour. 'You've learnt too much from your father.'

'Yes, Paul. I *have* learnt too much from my dear father.'

Stranger and stranger, he thought. No longer the loyal daughter.

'You—'

'Be it as it may, is that your final answer?' She posed the question over her shoulder as she walked towards the fireplace.

'Yes.'

'And that ... is the *wrong* answer.' She dropped her glass. It landed on an uncarpeted area – and shattered.

'What did you do that for?'

Lindsey feigned innocence. 'The glass? It was an accident.'

'No it wasn't.'

'Whatever.'

She stood stock still. There was no trace of the gratitude she had shown for him having saved her life. It looked as if she was waiting ... perhaps for him to yell at her? What was going through her head? Now that it was clear he wasn't interested in her offer, was she angling for a fight so that she could show him the door? He wouldn't give her the satisfaction.

A noise made him whip around.

A scream.

He froze. Michelle?

He started to run.

Paul stormed upstairs. Saw the study door was closed. All the doors were closed, apart from Bernard and Michelle's, which was halfway open. There was a light on.

He ran down the passage, pushed it open, burst inside.

Michelle was standing in the middle of the room, a man behind her, his forearm clasped around her throat.

Johnny.

He was holding something against her head. A gun.

'What—'

'You certainly took your time,' Johnny said derisively.

'What the hell?'

Paul saw Bernard lying on his back in bed, his position so odd that he realised the man's hands were tied behind him. His mouth was twisted and his chest was heaving from trying to get up, from struggling to see what was happening.

Michelle's expression was one of pure fear. She looked at Paul before her eyes moved towards the revolver. Her arms were slack by her sides. It seemed she wasn't getting enough air.

He wanted to go to her, but there was no way he could chance it.

'Can't you tell what the hell is going on, Paul?' Lindsey's voice. She was standing a few paces from him, dead calm.

Paul turned to face her. 'You're part of this? Of whatever it is going down here?'

It was as plain as daylight, but he had to hear it from her. This was Lindsey, after all, meek Lindsey who had never before looked at him with such icy eyes.

'Of whatever. It's a long story.' She put her hand into the left-hand pocket of her dressing gown and removed a pair of blue leather gloves. 'But we have plenty of time.'

As she pulled them on, she informed them, 'By the way, Mary won't be around to help you – Michelle took care of that, although she didn't realise it at the time.' She nodded at the other woman. 'That glass you took Mary contained more than just brandy.'

'You—' Michelle could manage just the one word through the pressure on her throat.

Lindsey was blind to it. 'Mary will remember she got it from *you*. And do you know why you gave her something to make her sleep? Do you know why, Paul? Michelle?'

She gestured to the briefcase on the floor. 'You wanted to steal it. And that brings us ... to the person who is the cause of all this.'

She looked at the man on the bed with loathing.

Paul wondered how he could ever have thought Michelle a good actress. *Here* was the Oscar-winner in this home. Anyone who could veil such hatred in constant sweet smiles and gentle manners deserved every acting prize out there.

'Lindsey ...' The voice didn't sound like Bernard's; it was too weak to belong to a man everyone obeyed.

'Your chance to talk has long gone,' she informed him.

'My girl, you—'

'Don't "my girl" me.' The fact that she didn't explode made it worse. Her self-control showed how much she had bottled up. 'You were supposed to have kicked the bucket long ago, "Daddy". Do you know when? You think you just slipped that day?' she asked. 'Oh no. I made it happen.'

Bernard reaches the top of the stairs. He is used to walking down them, knows instinctively how long it will take for his foot to land; then the slight give of the carpet under his shoe.

But today is different. His foot hooks on something.

He stumbles.

On fishing line.

It's just the two of them at home. Far out of sight, she's hunched up, with the end of the fishing line in her hand.

It was lying there, invisible, waiting to be pulled taut at the right moment, and that moment had just arrived.

All the colour drained from Bernard's face, yet he stared at his daughter with uncomprehending eyes. He didn't want to comprehend.

Paul knew that feeling. Being trapped in a nightmare that could only get worse before it came to an end. But this was reality, this was *here*, and Bernard had no means of eventual escape.

Violence. He, Paul Mullan, couldn't get away from it. He had identified with it as a child, and since then it had followed him like a dog that wanted attention and would bite if none was given. He was not one of those people who ended up in the wrong place at the wrong time. It was fated that he would be here. All the hate in this house had waited for him to arrive so that it could finally boil over.

Bernard swallowed. 'But—'

'You know why.' Lindsey's rage finally showed in her tone of voice. 'Over *her*.'

Paul remembered how he and Lindsey had walked through the vineyards. What she had sounded like when she told him how her mother had shot herself in the study.

Now her voice was even. 'It was *your* fault. It was because of *you*.'

Bernard shook his head, a defensive gesture rather than a denial.

'You were supposed to die then. On the stairs. She's gone and here *you* still are. But now it's time.'

Johnny looked at the young woman with respect, almost admiration. Were they just working together, or sharing a bed as well?

'Lindsey,' Michelle managed, 'it's not too late. Stop!'

'She's right.' Even though it was part of Paul's past life, he *had* talked people out of doing stupid things. He gestured towards Bernard. 'You've had your revenge. Enough, Lindsey. His life will never be the same again.' He wanted to believe he sounded logical, like a reasonable person. 'Michelle and I won't say a thing about this. We'll just leave.'

'I'd thought you were going to do that this morning. With the money. I heard how much, the day before yesterday.' Lindsey looked at Bernard. 'While you were in the study. You and Rodrigo. I was at the door.'

Paul remembered what Bernard told him the man had said when he handed over the briefcase.

Here is the three point two you've been carrying on about.

Ernesto Rodrigo, dead now, and who had never been a part of this affair.

'As for the "bomb",' Lindsey continued, 'there had been a chance you'd see it didn't mean much, Paul. But you clearly weren't in the bomb unit when you were with the cops. Do you know how easy it is to hire an expert in just about anything in this country of ours? An old pal of Johnny's. Someone fond enough of money to, for example, help "abduct" me.'

'You simply drove off with him after you left your car at the hotel—'

'Someone who knew enough about bombs and that kind of thing to make it look convincing,' she said. 'Who would also be able to see to it that the scene looked right when the time came.'

And Paul could imagine it, how they got ready for him and Michelle to arrive at that factory. The man tying up Lindsey's wrists and ankles, fastening the grey box to her chest, the green and red wires.

'When I heard you approaching ...'

She must have pricked her ears for the sound of people coming inside. Heard him calling. Waited.

'... and I could activate it myself.'

The button was high up on the box, she'd have been able to push it with her chin. How many minutes would it count down? Four?

'And Paul, do you know what would have happened if you'd cut the other wire, the green one? The device wouldn't have exploded *either*. You would also have thought you'd made a smart choice.'

She'd had plenty of time to plan it, he realised. Time and hate and patience. The plan was just adjusted when he arrived on the scene.

'But that was all just in case. You were supposed to have taken off with the money. Then I would have "escaped" and come back here. It would,' and she looked at Bernard, 'have been the first of your punishments. For Michelle to have run away with Paul, for her to have chosen money and another man over you.

'But then they surprised me and saw it through.' She turned her head towards Michelle. 'And then—'

'Lindsey, please!' Michelle looked years older.

'The guy wasn't supposed to try to grab the briefcase from you. But money does strange things to people. You weren't supposed to shoot him either. Anyway, things worked out neatly in the end. Because now we're *here* ...'

Here it comes, thought Paul. He didn't know what, but something was on its way.

Excitement had broken through Lindsey's voice. The talking bit had to be just about over, the big reveal that had needed to be done so everyone could know how clever she was. Master of the situation. The foreplay.

She took a pistol out of her other pocket and passed it to Johnny so that he could press that to Michelle's head instead. She took the revolver from him, opened it up, kept talking as she removed five of the six rounds from the cylinder. 'Now there's something *you* need to do for us, Paul.'

She transferred the rounds to her pocket.

'What the fuck do you need me for?' Bile was rising in his throat. It was driving him crazy seeing Michelle this scared, but he was angry too. 'Seems like you can handle everything perfectly well yourself.'

'No. When it comes to certain matters, I need an aide.' Lindsey smiled at the man beside her. 'Like him. Johnny's faithful. Whether to me or to the money he's going to get, it doesn't matter.'

Lindsey set the revolver down on a shelf. 'Paul, you and Michelle knew about the money.'

She went over to the briefcase, opened it, pulled out a band of blue notes. 'You wanted to steal it.'

She let it fall.

'When Johnny and I woke up and got here, it had already happened. Look, there's still a bunch of notes lying on the carpet, you must have been in such a hurry. My poor father wanted to stop you.'

She picked up the revolver again, showed them the cylinder so they could see that there was one round left, closed it, spun the cylinder.

Vrrrrrrr.

She gestured to Johnny to stand aside and take her position. Now she was the one with the gun pressed to Michelle's head.

Johnny held the pistol out to Paul.

With her free hand Lindsey pointed to Bernard and said, 'And then, Paul, you shot him.'

53

He hadn't heard it wrong. It wasn't a joke. Those had been her words.

'Take it, hero.' Johnny was still holding the pistol out to him, those already small eyes narrowed to slits.

'Lindsey, you're insane!'

'That's debatable. Take it.'

Paul's hands turned hot and sweaty at the mere thought of even touching the weapon. 'It won't fit in with your story! If Bernard wanted to stop us, he would have had the pistol. It makes no sense if I shoot him.'

'You got it off him, that's all.' She sounded frighteningly calm. 'Shoot him – or I'll shoot her.' She pressed the barrel harder against Michelle's head.

'Lindsey!'

'Paul, you aren't here to *speak*.'

'Just listen!' he started.

'Looks like you think I'm kidding. Looks like you need some convincing.' Lindsey glared at him. Waited for him to react.

The seconds stretched out.

He was frozen.

Calmly, she curled her finger under the trigger. Pulled it.

Paul roared.

A click.

Michelle groaned.

It took a moment for him to realise she was still alive. The woman he loved was still here with him.

Paul's hand shook, his whole body was shaking, but now he took the pistol from Johnny.

Vrrrrrrr.

Lindsey had spun the cylinder again and snapped it shut so quickly that the barrel was back against Michelle's head.

'Don't think I have anything against you,' she told him. 'It's nothing personal. I just need you. But Paul, it *was* a mistake making such a bad choice. If you had wanted to be with me, everything would have been different.'

'Please,' said Michelle. 'Lindsey, please.'

'You need to say that to your boyfriend, not to me.'

Paul saw the dawning of another kind of betrayal on Bernard's face. Although given everything else that was happening, its significance was fleeting.

Lindsey smiled. 'Let's see how much he loves you, Michelle.'

'You're going to be so sorry about this later on,' Paul pleaded. 'Just think. Stop it.'

'Don't try your police psychology on me.' Her expression was as sneering as Johnny's; no wonder they'd recognised the latent viciousness in each other. 'But let me make it easier for you. Let me tell you what kind of man is lying in front of you.'

Bernard's mouth opened, as if he wanted to stop her.

Even though Lindsey's eyes were on him, they had lost their focus; she was seeing something else.

'That day we thought we were alone. We didn't realise my mother was already back from town ...'

The woman is in the upstairs passage, but not on her way to the study to shoot herself.

Not yet.

A beautiful woman, more than twenty years Bernard Russell's junior. And sometimes she gets depressed, but not today; in fact, she is feeling more cheerful than in quite some time.

Just before lunch she and Lindsey had been discussing what they would wear to next weekend's party in Cape Town. They had decided to have dresses made at the boutique that gave them such good service. Laughed as they quarrelled over who would wear which colour.

The kind of mother–daughter moment that made life bearable with a husband who once just had to have her but now no longer even noticed her.

Quite cheerful, yes.

When she enters her and her husband's bedroom, she sees them, beside each other.

No. It can't be. It's just her imagination ... and if she retraced her steps and came back in, the room would be empty.

Yet the scene remains unchanged. Bernard and her Lindsey – his Lindsey – in bed together, fear on their faces having swiftly replaced the lazy post-coital afterglow.

He is stretched out, his arm possessively draped over his daughter's young, firm stomach. But then they both jerk upright.

Lindsey wants to pull up the sheet, but can't, for Bernard is lying on top of it.

The woman swings around and leaves. Back in the passage she immediately knows what she has to do.

Now she heads for the study.

'Now you know, Paul.' Lindsey used her gun to point at Bernard. 'And Michelle, *this* is the man you wanted so badly. What happened between us was his decision. Here, in the bed you two share. His bed and my mother's. He decided it would be so, and I was an obedient daughter.'

Paul looked at Bernard. Who was looking away.

'So obedient that I didn't ask any questions,' Lindsey continued. 'He was my father. He was always right. So what we were doing was right too; it wouldn't matter what other people would think if they were to know.

'It was only when my mother shot herself that I understood how wrong it was. And then I started waiting. Stayed here, but waited. Paul, now you know everything. Do what you need to.'

'I …'

He looked at the firearm in his hand. It had already proved so thoroughly what it was capable of – taking the life of Lindsey's mother, and of the man that morning.

'It's him or Michelle. Easy choice, I'd say.'

'Why don't *you* shoot him?' Michelle asked.

'Oh.' Lindsey shrugged. 'I was waiting for the right way. This is the right way. It's Paul's job. Paul, who chose so unfortunately a short while ago. Go on, Paul.'

The pistol weighed a ton. He stared at Michelle ahead of him. He had to save her – she'd done nothing wrong. They were going to have a long, full life together.

Bernard was someone who deserved …

But he was a human being. And therefore he kept trying, kept looking for a way out. 'If Michelle were shot with a revolver, how could that be explained away? Who would have shot her, and why?'

For a moment Lindsey looked uncertain. 'It …' Then she became furious. 'It was yours. Don't try to confuse me!'

She returned the gun to Michelle's head.

He wanted to stop her but couldn't.

Wanted to shoot Bernard and stop her that way, but couldn't.

Lindsey looked at him expectantly.

He was sweating profusely, trying to ignore his increasing nausea.

Lindsey raised her eyebrows. She saw he wasn't going to do it and pulled the trigger.

A lifetime in that moment.

Click.

And, like lightning, *vrrrrrrr*, she spun the cylinder again and had the barrel back in place.

He *couldn't* allow her to pull the trigger again. It happened in threes, things like this. Everyone knew this.

He raised the object of death. Swung his arm towards Bernard.

'Paul ...' The man's voice was all but gone. Bernard Russell – businessman, farm owner, employer – shattered. Resigned to his fate.

You need to decide. And quickly. You grasp the pistol.

Lift it up.

Curl your finger around the trigger.

This is to save Mike.

You shoot. Your arm recoils.

A double echo.

And here he was again. Nobody else could save Michelle.

Bernard was corrupt and had corrupted everything he touched.

He had the pistol pointed directly at him, he wouldn't miss, despite the way his arm was shaking; he hadn't been the best shot in his unit for nothing.

Bernard's forehead.

He had been called to this. It was determined the day Paul Mullan was born. He would have to live with this too. Mike Wilkins had been a dry run.

But.

He wasn't the same person anymore. Now he knew it for a fact. Because he couldn't pull the trigger.

'One,' said Lindsey. 'Two.'

She wouldn't have a problem firing.

'Two and a half …'

She made a show of removing and replacing her trigger finger.

'Two and three quarters. Paul, you need to stop me, remember. You know what to do. Two and seven eighths. And …'

She pulled the trigger.

Click.

Someone moaned.

Him.

He dropped the pistol.

'I'm sorry,' he said to Michelle. 'I can't.'

Her eyes were still wild, but she nodded. She understood.

Hard sounds of frustration, aggression, from Lindsey. She would kill the woman he loved. It was as good as if it was his hand holding the revolver.

But she let go of Michelle. She leaned over, picked the pistol up from the floor, stood back.

One shot. Ear-splitting.

Two echoes followed.

Only then did Paul realise what had happened.

He grabbed his stomach with both hands. As if from afar came the realisation that the pain was not yet as bad as it would become. This was what he had been taught back in his police days: that shock usually prevents a gunshot victim from feeling the full impact of the pain immediately. Already, though, it felt as if a hyena were tearing at his innards. He staggered to the bed, nearly landing on top of Bernard, who made no sound, whose face no longer registered anything.

A scream.

'Michelle.' His lips formed her name but no sound came out.

She was gasping for breath.

The duvet underneath Paul was turning red. He kept his hands over the wound.

'Now you listen hard,' ordered Lindsey. She sighed. 'Okay, so it hasn't worked out the way I thought it would.'

Johnny tried to interrupt. 'But Lindsey—'

'That's life. I'm not so heartless that everyone need die. You can leave.'

'What?' asked Michelle, in a state of disbelief. 'You—'

'Don't make me change my mind.' Lindsey pointed at Paul. 'Help him.'

Then Michelle was by his side, her arms under his shoulder blades, pulling him up.

The pain increased, but he managed to stand, biting his lower lip in the effort so hard that it started to bleed.

'Go now.' Then Lindsey pointed at the briefcase. 'Take it. Your things and Michelle's are packed up and in Paul's room. You'll have to walk by yourself. She can't carry everything *and* hold you up.'

Michelle let go of him, leaned over and picked up the briefcase.

'Get to a doctor with that gunshot wound, and soon,' said Lindsey. 'The bullet is from this pistol – the one that,' and she pointed at Bernard, 'will be discovered in *his* hand.'

Johnny was upset that they'd be getting away. 'You can't ...'

'It's the right thing to do it myself,' said Lindsey. 'For me. For my mother.'

She appeared to want to move, but didn't.

Before he and Michelle turned to walk away, Paul saw the icy look melt from her face and her bearing grow less certain.

A small child stood in her place. Deserted.

54

The night air was wet and damp against his cheeks. The moon was bright. Paul didn't know how he ... how they had made it out there. Out of the corner of his eye he saw something dark moving, something they had frightened and that was flying away now. Must have been an owl.

Michelle helped him into the front of the red Citi Golf. She opened her mouth, wanting to speak.

Before she had time, though, a distinct sound pierced the air. A gunshot. Paul realised they had left the front door open.

Echo, echo.

For a moment he thought there had been a second shot. But it was the car door Michelle had slammed. Even so, he blacked out.

When he came round, Michelle was driving, and not on an uneven dirt road.

His stomach – how much blood had he lost? A new wave of pain radiated from his middle. He groaned.

'Are you with me again?' She looked at him and he could hear how concerned she was, just how upset. 'How bad is the pain?'

'I feel like I'm dying.'

'You'll live. I think I'd know a fatal wound if I saw one. But we need to get you to a doctor. God knows where.' She glanced in the rear-view mirror.

'Don't look back,' he told her.

'Look ahead, huh?' She went quiet, but not for long. 'Remember when you said you were yearning for a new beginning? Well, let's go look for ours. And don't forget, there's a briefcase full of money on the seat behind us …'

And she was right. It was as good a beginning as two people could expect. Love, a ride and some money.

As for that feeling he'd had that there could be no happy ending for them?

Sometimes you just had to ignore things like that.

R46

Hermon	9
(R44) Wellington	32
Ceres	63